PRAISE FOR ANNA CAMPBELL

"*The Seduction of Lord Stone* is romantic, emotional, sexy and funny. In fact, everything I have come to expect from Anna Campbell. I'm looking forward to reading the other Dashing Widows' stories." —*RakesandRascals.com*

"With her marvelous combination of humor and poignancy Anna Campbell writes in such a way that every story of hers has a special meaning and remains like a sentimental keepsake with those fortunate enough to read her work!" —*JeneratedReviews.com*

"*Lord Garson's Bride* is a well written and passionate story that touched my heart and sent my emotions on a rollercoaster ride. I particularly recommend this book for fans of convenient marriages, and those who enjoy seeing a deserving character find out that love is lovelier the second time around." —*Roses Are Blue Reviews*

"Campbell immediately hooks readers, then deftly reels them in with a spellbinding love story fueled by an addictive mixture of sharp wit, lush sensuality, and a wealth of well-delineated characters."—*Booklist, starred review, on A Scoundrel by Moonlight*

"With its superbly nuanced characters, impeccably crafted historical setting, and graceful writing shot through with scintillating wit, Campbell's latest lusciously sensual, flawlessly written historical Regency ... will have romance readers sighing happily with satisfaction."—*Booklist, Starred Review, on What a Duke Dares*

"Campbell makes the Regency period pop in the appealing third Sons of Sin novel. Romantic fireworks, the constraints of custom, and witty banter are combined in this sweet and successful story."—*Publishers Weekly on What a Duke Dares*

"Campbell is exceptionally talented, especially with plots that challenge the reader, and emotions and characters that are complex and memorable."—*Sarah Wendell, Smart Bitches Trashy Books, on A Rake's Midnight Kiss*

"A lovely, lovely book that will touch your heart and remind you why you read romance."—*Liz Carlyle, New York Times bestselling author on What a Duke Dares*

"Campbell holds readers captive with her highly intense, emotional, sizzling and dark romances. She instinctually knows how to play on her readers' fantasies to create a romantic, deep-sigh tale."—*RT Book Reviews, Top Pick, on Captive of Sin*

"Don't miss this novel - it speaks to the wild drama of the heart, creating a love story that really does transcend class."—*Eloisa James, New York Times bestselling author, on Tempt the Devil*

"*Seven Nights in A Rogue's Bed* is a lush, sensuous treat. I was enthralled from the first page to the last and still wanted more."—*Laura Lee Guhrke, New York Times bestselling author*

"No one does lovely, dark romance or lovely, dark heroes like Anna Campbell. I love her books."— *Sarah MacLean, New York Times bestselling author*

"It isn't just the sensuality she weaves into her story that makes Campbell a fan favorite, it's also her strong, three-dimensional characters, sharp dialogue and deft plotting. Campbell intuitively knows how to balance the key elements of the genre and give readers an irresistible, memorable read."—*RT Book Reviews, Top Pick, on Midnight's Wild Passion*

"Anna Campbell is an amazing, daring new voice in romance."—*Lorraine Heath, New York Times bestselling author*

"Ms. Campbell's gorgeous writing a true thing of beauty..."—*Joyfully Reviewed*

ALSO BY ANNA CAMPBELL

Claiming the Courtesan

Untouched

Tempt the Devil

Captive of Sin

My Reckless Surrender

Midnight's Wild Passion

The Sons of Sin series:

Seven Nights in a Rogue's Bed

Days of Rakes and Roses

A Rake's Midnight Kiss

What a Duke Dares

A Scoundrel by Moonlight

Three Proposals and a Scandal

The Dashing Widows:

The Seduction of Lord Stone

Tempting Mr. Townsend

Winning Lord West

Pursuing Lord Pascal

Charming Sir Charles

Catching Captain Nash

Lord Garson's Bride

The Lairds Most Likely:

The Laird's Willful Lass

The Laird's Christmas Kiss

The Highlander's Lost Lady

Christmas Stories:

The Winter Wife

Her Christmas Earl

A Pirate for Christmas

Mistletoe and the Major

A Match Made in Mistletoe

The Christmas Stranger

Other Books:

These Haunted Hearts

Stranded with the Scottish Earl

THE SEDUCTION OF LORD STONE

THE DASHING WIDOWS BOOK 1

ANNA CAMPBELL

 Serenade Publishing

Print editions published by Serenade Publishing
www.serenadepublishing.com

Thanks to Ann, Christine and Sharon for going above and beyond.

PROLOGUE

Grosvenor Square, London, February 1820

The world expected a widow to be sad.

The world expected a widow to be lonely.

The world didn't expect a widow to be bored to the point of throwing a brick through a window, just to shatter the endless monotony of her prescribed year of mourning.

Outside the opulent drawing room, fashionable Grosvenor Square presented a bleak view. Leafless trees, gray skies, people scurrying past wrapped up beyond recognition as they rushed to be indoors again. Even inside, the winter air kept its edge. The bitter weather reflected the chill inside Caroline, Lady Beaumont; the endless fear that she sacrificed her youth to stultifying convention. She sighed heavily and flattened one palm on the cold glass, wondering if there would always be a barrier between her and freedom.

"You're out of sorts today, Caro," Fenella, Lady Deerham, said softly from where she presided over the tea table. While Caroline was this afternoon's hostess, habit—and good sense—saw Fenella dispensing refreshments. She was neat and efficient in her movements, unlike Caroline who tended to gesticulate when something caught her attention. Fenella would never spill tea over the priceless Aubusson carpet.

"It's so blasted miserable out there." Caroline still stared discontentedly at the deserted square. "I don't think I've seen the sun in three months."

"Now, you know that's an exaggeration," Helena, Countess of Crewe, said from the gold brocade sofa beside the roaring fire.

How like Helena to stick to facts. On their first meeting, this intellectual, sophisticated woman had terrified Caroline. She'd since learned to appreciate Helena's incisive mind and plain speaking—most of the time.

Nor would anyone have predicted Caroline's friendship with Fenella. Fenella was gentle and sweet, and at first, Caroline had dismissed her as a bit of a fool. But after a year's acquaintance, she recognized Fenella's kindness as strength not weakness, a strength that threw an unforgiving light on her own occasional lack of generosity.

She'd met Helena Wade and Fenella Deerham at one of the dull all-female gatherings designated suitable entertainment for women grieving the loss of a spouse. Their youth—all three were under thirty—had drawn them together rather than any immediate affinity. But somehow, despite their differences, or perhaps because of them, Caroline now counted these two disparate ladies as her closest friends.

With another sigh, Caroline turned to face the room. "I doubt I'd have survived my mourning without you two."

Helena paused in sipping her tea, her striking dark-eyed face with its imperious Roman nose expressing puzzlement. "That sounds discomfitingly like a farewell. Do you plan to abandon us for more exciting company once your official year is up?"

Fenella regarded Helena with rare reproach. "Don't tease her. She's only saying what's true for all of us."

"Exactly, Fen." Caroline sent the pretty blonde in the plain gray dress a grateful smile. "Trust our resident dragon to puncture my sentimental bubble."

Helena, slender and elegant in her widow's weeds—Caroline envied her friend's ability to create style from crepe and bombazine—watched her thoughtfully, not noticeably gratified by the declaration. "Nonetheless your seclusion ends next month. No wonder you're champing at the bit."

Horsy terms littered Helena's conversation. She was by reputation a punishing rider, although bereavement had curtailed her exercise.

"Aren't you?" Caroline crossed to extend her delicate Meissen cup for more tea.

"Devoting a year of my life to the memory of a brute like Crewe is hypocritical at the very least. Not to mention an infernal waste of time in the saddle."

"Seclusion must chafe when you didn't love your husband," Caroline said, taking a sip.

Helena's gaze didn't waver. "You didn't love yours either."

Caroline wanted to protest, but the sad truth was that Helena was right. Freddie had been a stranger when she'd married him, and their years together hadn't done much to increase the intimacy. Marriage was a cruel yoke, uniting such an incompatible pair. Even crueler that she'd been forced to follow Freddie's dictates as to where they lived and what they did. Mourning him was the last obligation she owed her late husband. Once the year was over, she meant to enjoy her independence and never surrender it again.

"Helena!" Fenella said repressively as she refilled the other cups. "We both know Caro was fond of Beaumont."

Helena's laugh was grim. "The way she's fond of a dog, Fen?"

In the stark afternoon light, Fenella's beauty was ethereal. "You're unkind."

Helena shook her glossy dark head. "No, I'm honest. Surely after all these months, it's time we spoke openly to one another." A trace of warmth softened her cool, precise voice. "Because you've both proven my salvation, too. I would have run mad without you to remind me that other people have feelings, Fen. Caro, I never have to pretend with you. And for some reason you both seem to like me anyway."

Helena generally steered clear of emotion. This was the closest she'd ever ventured to confidences. Surprised, Caroline studied her, seeing more than she ever had before. At last, she glimpsed the deep reserves of feeling lurking beneath that self-assured exterior.

"Mostly," she said in a dry tone, knowing Helena would take the response the way it was meant.

"So did you love Frederick Beaumont?" Helena persisted.

Poor Freddie, saddled with a weak constitution and an unloving helpmeet. Hatred would have been a greater tribute than his wife's indifference. How sad for a decent, if tedious man to die so young. Sadder that nobody in particular cared that he'd gone.

"No," she said hollowly, at last voicing the shameful truth. "Although he was a good man, and he deserved better from me than he got."

Freddie should have married a stolid farmer's wife, not a restless, curious, volatile creature who dreamed of the social whirl instead of milk yields and barley prices. By the end of Caroline's ten years in Lincolnshire, she'd felt like she drowned in mud. She sucked in a breath of London air, reminding herself that now she was free.

"Crewe deserved considerably less than he got from me," Helena said sourly. "He wasn't even any good in bed. If a woman must wed a degenerate rake, the least she should expect is physical satisfaction."

Fenella was blushing. She always looked about sixteen when she was embarrassed. "Well, I loved Henry. And he loved me." She sounded uncharacteristically defiant. "I'll always miss him."

Fenella's happy marriage always filled Caroline with a mixture of envy and disbelief—and guilt that she couldn't mourn Freddie with an ounce of the same sincerity. But if she needed an example of the dangers of a close union, she merely needed to glimpse the sorrow in Fen's fine blue eyes.

Helena regarded Fenella with fond impatience. "You were lucky to have a good man, Fen. But Waterloo was five years ago, and you're still wearing half mourning. Isn't it time to start living again?"

Fenella paled at Helena's unprecedented candor. She rarely encountered a word of criticism. Caroline had long ago noticed that Fenella's air of fragility made people treat her like glass, ready to shatter at the slightest rough treatment.

"You don't understand. It's different for me," Fenella stammered.

"Because of your son?" Caroline asked, wondering

for the thousandth time how different her marriage might have been if God had granted her children. Would she have felt so trapped, so frustrated, so useless? Who knew?

"Brandon's only ten. He needs me."

"And you're only twenty-nine," Helena retorted. "You need to look for love again."

"I don't want love," Fenella said stiffly. She bit her lip and turned a tragic gaze on her friends. "It hurts too much to lose it."

With that stark statement, confirming Caroline's doubts about even a loving marriage, the spate of confidences slammed to a shuddering halt. A desolate silence descended on the luxurious room. Only the crackling fire and a spatter of raindrops on the windows broke the quiet.

Eventually Helena smiled, but Caroline saw the effort it took. "I'm sorry, Fen. I'm as blue-deviled as Caro. It must be the weather. I have no right to harangue you."

Caroline gestured, sloshing her tea into the saucer, and spoke with sudden urgency. "We all have the right to offer our opinion. It's what people do when they care."

Annoyance banished Fenella's distress, thank goodness. For a few moments there, Caroline had worried that her usually serene friend might dissolve into tears. "So you too believe I should forget the best person I've ever known, a faithful husband, a loving father, a brave soldier?"

For safety's sake, Caroline set her cup on the tea table before she slid into the chair beside Fenella's. When she took Fenella's hand, she wasn't surprised to find it trembling. "You'll never forget him. And neither you should. But Henry wouldn't want you to hide away from the outside world, not when you're young and beautiful with so much to give. The man you've described would never be so mean spirited."

Fenella's grip tightened. "I'm not brave like you and Helena. I'm comfortable in my rut. The truth is that I'm afraid of facing the world again, especially without Henry by my side."

"It's brave to admit your fear," Helena said from the sofa in an unusually subdued voice. "And you're wrong about my courage. I might act as if I'm ready to take on the world, but I've already had one disastrous marriage. Choosing a pig like Crewe, especially when I defied my parents to have him, puts my judgment in serious question."

"Oh, Helena." Fenella's lovely face softened with compassion. "You've learned from your mistakes. And you were so young then."

"We were all young," Caroline said in a low voice. "We're still young."

Freddie had been young, too. But at least he'd led the life he chose. Until illness struck him down, he'd been blissfully happy in the muck and mire of his fields. Caroline realized that if she died tomorrow, she'd never done a single thing she wanted. That seemed even more of a waste than Freddie's lingering death. She'd devoted three long years to nursing him. She'd emerged from those harrowing days painfully aware of life's brevity and how easily the years could slip away with nothing to show for them but drudgery.

"What about you, Caro?" Helena asked. "This gray day has us stripping our souls bare. We've started telling the truth. We may as well continue. What frightens you?"

Gathering her dark, confused thoughts, Caroline stared blindly into the fire. Pictures from the barren past filled her mind. Her austere girlhood, the only child of elderly parents with rigid ideas of behavior. Her seventeen-year-old self marrying stodgy, tongue-tied Freddie Beaumont with not a shred of romance to brighten the occasion. Ten dreary years as a farming baronet's wife in wet, windy Lincolnshire, with no company but the equally dreary neighbors and a prize dairy herd. This last uneventful year in London as she waited out her period of mourning for a man who had left little impression on her, however much she might pity his untimely death.

"Caro?" Fenella prompted gently. "Helena's right. If we can't be candid with one another, who can we be candid with?"

Caroline swallowed to shift the boulder of emotion jamming her throat. Guilt at not grieving for Freddie as a wife should. Lifelong dissatisfaction. A burning need to forge her own path. She loathed the restrictions of mourning. To use Helena's terminology, she'd kicked against convention like a half-broken horse in a narrow stall.

But her festering restlessness had a deeper cause. She was no different to Fenella and Helena. She too was terrified. And the admission nearly choked her.

She straightened until her back was stiff as a ruler, the way she'd been trained to sit as a girl groomed to marry her father's wealthy godson Frederick Beaumont. "I dread that what's to come will be as dull as what's past. I dread that I'll die without ever having lived." She met her friends' eyes. "And I have a raging hunger for life."

"Oh, Caro." Fenella placed one arm around her shoulders and squeezed. "It's not too late."

"We all deserve some excitement," she said huskily, finding comfort in Fen's hug. "I feel like I've been locked away in the dark all my life. I've spent twenty-eight years waiting. I've never had a chance to laugh and dance and carry on romantic intrigues."

"What's stopping you now?" Helena asked. "You're beautiful and rich and ripe for adventure."

As her fretfulness drained away, Caroline dredged up a smile for her friend. Then the smile widened as she considered what Helena had said. Truly what was stopping her now? Nothing but cowardice. The fear of the unknown, even if what she'd known had made her feel buried alive.

Well, no longer. Her parents had gone. Freddie had gone. She remained, and it was up to her to seize her liberty with both hands. If she didn't, the only person she'd have to blame was herself.

She sucked in another breath, and for the first time in over a decade felt her lungs expand without restriction. On a sudden, intoxicating surge of hope, she rose from the spindly chair. "I'm definitely rich and ripe for adventure."

"Once you're out of mourning, you'll be the most dashing widow in London," Fenella said.

"I shall indeed."

Fenella smiled at her. "When you set your mind to something, you make sure you achieve it. I so admire your strength."

"My father called it blind stubbornness," she admitted. "He tried to beat it out of me, but he never did."

"Thank goodness," Helena said. "You wouldn't be nearly so interesting if you just accepted your fate. In fact, you'd still be wiping the mud off your shoes in Lincolnshire."

"I am determined to make a new life, one where the decisions are mine." Caroline shifted until she could see both women. "In fact, why don't we all leave our old, sad days behind? Why don't we all become dashing widows?"

Helena's dark eyes flared with excitement.

Predictably Fenella looked less enamored with the idea. "I can see you both dazzling the ton. I'm not like that."

Refusing to let Fen shrink back into her seclusion, Caroline caught her hands and hauled her to her feet. "You're the prettiest girl I know, Fenella Deerham. You'll dazzle the ton purely by turning up."

"I'm not sure," Fenella murmured.

Less impetuously, Helena stood and crossed the room to join them. "Don't you want to dance the night away and drink champagne and flirt with handsome gentlemen?"

Fenella still resisted the rising mood. "I don't want to marry again."

Caroline laughed, caught up in the idea of breaking free of stifling limitations. "Dashing widows don't have to marry. They've done their duty. Dashing widows have fun."

A reluctant smile tugged at Fenella's lips. "I can't remember the last time I had fun."

"There you are, then," Helena said. "We'll all be dashing widows."

With a giddy laugh, Caroline stepped across to ring for a servant. "We'll be the most dashing widows the ton has ever seen."

"Count me in," Helena said, and for once her expression held no trace of irony.

"Fen, you can't turn the terrible trio into a desperate duo," Caroline urged.

Fenella still looked unconvinced. "It's so long since I was out in society."

"I've never been out in society. My father wouldn't pay for a season when the match with Freddie was already arranged," Caroline said. "Helena will have to be our guide."

Helena's lips twitched. "Heaven help us, then." Earnestness deepened her voice. "Come and join us, Fen. We're not asking you to run a steeplechase in your petticoat. We're just inviting you to chance a step out of your safe little cave. You commit to nothing more than wearing colors and attending a party or two."

Something new sparked in Fenella's eyes, banishing her customary melancholy. She raised her chin with un-Fenella-like brio. "Very well. I'll do it."

"Wonderful," Helena said, hugging her with un-Helena-like exuberance.

The butler entered the room. Caroline greeted him with a smile and caught his surprise at the festive atmosphere. Another signal, should she need one, that it was time she crawled out of her slough of self-pity and made plans for her independence.

"Hunter, champagne."

"Caro, at five o'clock in the afternoon?" Fenella asked, shocked.

Hunter bowed, his imperturbability back in place. "Very good, my lady."

Caroline beamed, the pall of boredom and frustration shifting from her shoulders. She felt light enough to float up into the cloudy winter sky. From what she saw of her friends, they too had found fresh purpose on this February afternoon.

"Why not? Dashing widows drink champagne whenever they feel like it. What better excuse than a toast to our glittering success?"

CHAPTER ONE

May 1820

The Grosvenor Square house stood transformed. Spring had arrived and with it a release from the pall of mourning. Caroline had thrown herself wholeheartedly into the season, and tonight's ball was the culmination of her campaign to win society's acclaim.

She halted in the doorway to her crowded, noisy ballroom, at last able to catch a breath. Holding what turned out to be a brilliant success of a party required diligent attention. But finally, everything was in place and she was ready to have fun. The orchestra played a lively quadrille; a lavish supper was ready and under Hunter's capable supervision; she'd greeted all her guests, delighted at how many people had accepted her invitation. Of course society was curious about rich Lady Beaumont, so recently out of mourning. But she could see already that tonight curiosity veered toward approval.

Helena was dancing with a red-haired fellow whose name escaped her. Fenella danced, too, her pale prettiness flushed to vivacity. She wore a sky blue dress in the first stare of fashion—it was so pleasing to see her in something other than gray. Both friends had worked like Trojans with Caroline to ensure that the launch of the dashing widows was a triumph.

"You're looking revoltingly pleased with yourself, Caro," a deep voice murmured in her ear.

Pleasure warmed her and extending her hand, she turned with a smile. "Silas, I wasn't sure you'd tear yourself away from your greenhouses long enough to come."

Silas Nash, Viscount Stone, was Helena's older brother, the cleverest member of a notoriously clever family. Soon after coming to London, Caroline had met the noted botanist at Helena's house. She'd immediately liked his humor and kindness. And his handsomeness had offered a welcome distraction during the dull days of her seclusion. A handsomeness of which he remained refreshingly unaware.

"I wouldn't miss this for the world. You've arrived with fireworks." He bowed over her gloved hand, hazel eyes glinting up at her as he bent.

He always treated her as if they shared a joke that

the rest of the world had missed. It made her feel special. *He* made her feel special. When she came to London, unhappy and uncertain, she'd been deeply grateful for his support. Tonight, happy and confident, she remained deeply grateful. "Helena has been talking."

He straightened and released her hand. "Perhaps she dropped a hint here and there about the evening's finale."

She couldn't contain a smug smile. "My party is a great success, isn't it?"

"It is indeed." He regarded her from under tawny eyebrows, his gaze sharp. "I congratulate you on your victory over society."

She flicked her fan open and cast him a flirtatious glance as she fell into their familiar bantering. "I intend to enjoy myself."

"You deserve to kick up your heels a little." The fondness in his expression made her heart swell. She wondered if he knew quite how much his friendship meant to her. His immediate approbation had done wonders for her self-assurance when she'd been new in Town. Without it, she doubted she'd have had the nerve to claim a prominent place in the ton.

"Oh, I plan on doing more than a little," she said on a laugh. "I've spent my life as someone's dutiful daughter or someone's obedient wife. Now I seek amusement on my own account—and nobody can say me nay."

"Until you find another husband."

All the color and music and movement around her jangled into cacophony in her head. Her throat clogged with horror. Another husband? She'd rather die.

"Caro?"

Silas's voice brought her back, reminded her that she need never enter the smothering hell of married life again. Instead, here she was with handsome Silas Nash, and she was free to enjoy herself precisely how she wished.

She took in the tall, rangy build set off to perfection in evening clothes, the thick honey-brown hair, his intense, intelligent face with its Roman nose so like Helena's. It all made for a man of more than average appeal. His title was singularly inappropriate—anyone less like a stone was impossible to imagine. He was the most alive person she'd ever met.

She waved her fan slowly in front of her face, chasing off all her dark memories. Tonight was hers, and she didn't intend to waste it on unhappy thoughts. "I don't want another husband."

He frowned. "Of course you do."

"Of course I don't." She tilted her chin and took advantage of the small island of privacy surrounding them to confide her wicked intentions. "I am, however, in the market for a lover."

As she'd expected, her pronouncement didn't shock Silas. His tolerant attitude was among the many things she liked about him. He regarded her thoughtfully. "Is that an invitation, Caro?"

She stared into his unwavering hazel eyes. Around her, the crowded ballroom receded strangely until she and Silas seemed alone together.

Caroline hadn't blushed since before she'd married Freddie. But something in Silas's expression brought color to her cheeks and a disconcerting stumble to her heart. Which was absurd. Even without Helena's warnings—and her friend had early dampened any thought of setting her cap at Silas—she'd soon recognized that he never took his conquests seriously. While for all their shared jokes, she did take this friendship seriously.

When she'd mentally listed the men she'd consider inviting to her bed, she hadn't included Silas. She couldn't bear for him to dismiss her the way he dismissed all his flirts beyond the immediate seduction.

And if he didn't dismiss her, what then? She didn't want anything that required a commitment. As she'd told Silas, she was never going to marry again. Tiptoeing around Freddie's feelings had been hard enough. Catering to a man who loved her, a man she wanted to please, was signing up for another life sentence.

Far better Silas remained her dear friend, and she sought physical pleasure elsewhere.

After a month in society, she'd seen enough to know that a dashing widow would easily find a lover.

Replacing a true friend was an entirely different matter. Which meant she stalwartly ignored the unprecedented catch in her breath when Silas focused that green-gold stare on her. Even if he looked like he'd need little encouragement to sweep her off and prove his reputation as a devil with the ladies.

"I'm more than you can handle," she said lightly with a flutter of her fan. "You like them silly and flighty. Neither word applies to me."

His mouth firmed when she'd hoped to make him smile. "That sounds like a challenge."

Startled, she looked at him properly. Their interactions were usually unshadowed, a blessing in a world that had varied between black and gray as long as hers had. She'd imagined, once she left her seclusion behind, that the easy camaraderie would continue. Perhaps she'd been naive.

He looked disgruntled. It took her so long to interpret the expression because she'd never seen it on his face before. Sulking sat surprisingly well on Silas's vivid features. Which obscurely annoyed her more than it should.

No woman could miss how attractive Silas was, but so far, she'd admired his spectacular looks as one might admire a fine painting. A brooding Lord Stone became unacceptably compelling. She forced a laugh and wished she sounded more natural. She snapped her fan shut and tapped him on the arm. "You're teasing."

Still he didn't smile. "Am I?"

A horrible thought arose, scattering her archness. "Good God, Silas, don't say you disapprove of my plans? I never imagined you'd be mealy mouthed about a few adventures, not when you've been mad for the girls since you went to Cambridge."

The grim expression didn't lighten. She'd never seen him so stern. "Apparently Helena's been spreading tales about more than this evening's entertainments."

His unfavorable reaction left her flummoxed. Lord Stone's beautiful manners were touted as society's ideal. His careless wit and graceful demeanor were much praised. Yet he responded now with neither wit nor grace, when she'd expected him to applaud her daring.

Caroline became annoyed. With Silas Nash, of all people. "I was a good and faithful wife to Frederick Beaumont. And I nearly perished of boredom as a result. If I choose to take a lover or two now, it's entirely my decision. If that doesn't fit some hypocritical view you have of respectable women, that's too bad. I won't apologize."

She waited for him to respond with equal heat, but after a fraught second while she braced for a scolding, he sucked in a breath and the temper faded from his expression. "Let's not quarrel, Caro. Not tonight when you're basking in your success."

"Your censure oversteps the mark, my lord," she said stiffly, telling herself to accept his olive branch.

But worse than anger, she was hurt that someone she'd counted as an ally turned against her.

His lips quirked and abruptly he became the easy-going companion who had helped her weather all those humdrum tea parties. "'My lord?' Oh, the pain. I'll never recover. You know how to strike a man down, Lady Beaumont."

Despite her disquiet, she couldn't suppress a faint smile. "I probably shouldn't have told you my plans. I've become too used to confiding in you." She studied him searchingly. "If I lost your regard, I'd be cast low indeed."

He expelled his breath with a hint of impatience. "Don't be a goose, Caro. You haven't lost my regard. You never could." He glanced around the packed room. "I'll prove it by asking you to dance."

The familiar benevolence settled on his features, but she hadn't mistaken his anger in those brief moments of discord. She battled the uncomfortable suspicion that she didn't know Silas Nash at all.

"I must check on the supper," she said quickly, although it wasn't true. She needed to gather her composure. Their discussion had come too close to argument and left her on edge. Fear beat in her blood, chilled her on this warm night. If Silas withdrew his friendship, she'd miss him like the devil.

"Given the interest our contretemps has aroused, a waltz would be the wiser choice."

She started. Good heavens. What on earth was

wrong with her? She'd forgotten where she was. She'd taken so much trouble to establish herself in society. Now in bickering with a rake, she risked all she'd gained. A quick reconnoiter indicated more than one pair of eyes focused on her. She caught Helena's concerned dark gaze and sent her a reassuring smile.

"You're right," she said, still reluctant to step into Silas's arms for the dance. Then she squared her shoulders and damned the world, and Lord Stone with it. She'd lived too long as a mouse. Now she meant to be a tiger.

"Shall we?"

The orchestra she'd brought from Paris played the introduction to the latest waltz. Ignoring the disquiet churning in her stomach, Caroline stuck a brilliant smile on her face and nodded. "We shall."

∾

And that, sir, was how *not* to court a lady.

What a blockhead he was. Silas had known from the moment he met beautiful and stubborn Caroline Beaumont that if he intended to win her, he needed to tread carefully.

For over a year, he, famous for his various but fleeting amours, had done just that. Until now, he'd never taken trouble over a woman. If the one who caught his fickle interest wouldn't have him—and he was arrogant enough to note how rarely that happened

—there was always another equally appealing candidate to occupy his brief attention.

Then his brilliant, troublesome, but beloved sister Helena had held a tea party on a cold March day. His wayward attention had landed on a lovely woman whose fiery spirit made a mockery of her widow's weeds. He'd spent every day since then telling himself that love at first sight was a poet's stupidity—and eating his heart out over Caro Beaumont. For a man of thirty-one, it was distinctly lowering to suffer romantic yearnings that rivaled any adolescent Romeo's. Even more lowering to recognize that the object of his inconvenient passion hardly regarded him as a man at all.

Payment, he supposed, for all those casually discarded ladies.

He curled one arm around Caro's slender waist and took her gloved hand in his, and his heart leaped with an excitement he hadn't felt since he was a stripling. It was humiliating. It was disturbing. It was unacceptable.

And after this long enchantment, he acknowledged that it was inescapable.

Since she'd cast off her mourning, he'd danced with her several times. Usually she was light and supple in his arms, responding to his body's signals with a readiness that boded well for her bedding. Now tension stiffened the delicate muscles beneath his hand.

Blast. Impatience had brought him close to blowing his plans. Caro did a fine job of pretending enjoyment, but he saw beneath the sparkling surface to the old wariness. From the first, she'd been skittish. Like a highly strung thoroughbred mistreated early and as a result, disinclined to trust to any handler, even the kindest. How she'd loathe knowing that Silas had immediately recognized her fear—she was a proud creature, as befitted a thoroughbred, and worthy of a gentle wooing.

Damn it, he verged so close, yet he could still lose the prize. How far the rake had fallen that he'd counted gaining her trust as a victory. He'd built that trust step by step, through a hundred innocuous gatherings suitable for a new widow.

He never ventured into deeper waters with Caroline. Instead, he'd set out to make her laugh—some instinct told him laughter had been a rare visitor to her life. In return she'd gifted him with a friendship that, to his shame, counted as his most rewarding relationship with a female outside his family.

Tonight, like a fathead, he'd put all that dedicated hard work at risk.

But dear God, he'd wanted to smash his fist into the wall when, after a year without so much as a kiss, she spoke in such an offhand manner about taking a lover. A lover who was not Silas Nash, Viscount Stone.

"Silas, you're holding me too tightly."

He emerged from his fit of the sullens—confound it, no woman but Caro pierced his sangfroid—to find her watching him curiously. And with more of that dashed wariness.

Careful, Silas.

He made himself smile and loosened the hand clutching her waist the way a falling man clutched an overhang on a mountainside. "My apologies."

He'd imagined that their friendship would offer him some advantage over other predatory males. Now he wondered if he'd made a basic mistake in his strategy. He'd become part of the furniture of her life, when she was on the hunt for novelty and excitement.

His fear of competition was well founded. In this room a host of men, good and bad, watched the beautiful widow with avid eyes. He could hardly blame them. In unrelieved black, she'd been lovely. In a red gown with gold embroidery and a décolletage that skimmed the edges of propriety—and a few other things—she was breathtaking. With difficulty, Silas kept his attention on her face and not on the wealth of white skin displayed below her collarbones.

As he whirled her around the room, her smile became more natural. "No, I'm sorry. I spoke inappropriately. It's partly your fault. You've become a mainstay of my life since I came to London. Like Helena or Fenella."

Bugger him to hell and back. He only just hid a wince. "I don't want to see you hurt."

Which was true, if not the whole truth. He intended to be the man to introduce her to sensual delight. She'd only ever mentioned her married life in passing. But hints—and the few stultifyingly dull occasions when he'd met Freddie Beaumont, a good soul, but as thick-witted as a sheep—had led him to some interesting conclusions about her sexual experience. She was ripe with womanly promise, but every instinct screamed that all her bottled-up passion had never yet found outlet.

His declaration left her unmoved. "I intend to have some fun, Silas. I'm not looking for anything significant."

He knew it was a mistake to ask. What point torturing himself? And worse, inviting another set-down. "Have you decided on a lucky candidate?"

For a second, he worried that he'd betrayed how important her answer was. But after a pause, she responded. "A few gentlemen have caught my interest."

He sucked in a relieved breath. She hadn't made her choice yet, so the affair remained in the realm of theory.

She lowered her voice. "Lord West is a most charming gentleman."

Shock made Silas trip, he who had learned to dance at eight years old and hadn't made a misstep since.

"West?" he choked out, forgetting all his plans for a subtle pursuit. Luckily his inamorata watched that popinjay West waltz with Helena a few feet away. Caro was too distracted to notice that her dance partner contemplated murder.

"We've met several times. He's articulate and handsome and seems considerate."

The unconcealed interest in her dark blue eyes threatened to make Silas lose his dinner. In an attempt to rein in his explosive reactions, he looked at Vernon Grange, Baron West, the man he'd previously considered his best friend. "Until he moves on to his next mistress. West has an appalling reputation with women."

"That's the pot calling the kettle black," she retorted.

He looked down into Caro's piquant face under the elaborate coronet of dark brown curls set with glittering diamond pins. His darling was no fragile beauty like her friend Fenella Deerham. Her face was too angular and full of character to be fashionably pretty. But the sight of her transformed his day from the mundane to the extraordinary.

And she talked about wasting herself on that scoundrel West.

Silas told himself that a short affair with another man didn't toll a death knell to his dreams. But everything male roared denial. Silas didn't want Caro Beaumont in West's bed. He wanted her in *his* bed. For always.

With difficulty, he found the rhythm of the music again. "He'll leave you once he's bored—and that usually means after only a few weeks."

She was back to regarding him like a complete

stranger, blast her. "Stone, I'm contemplating a fling, not lifelong slavery."

Slavery? What a clod he was. Finally and reluctantly, he recognized that her opposition to a second marriage was real—and deep-seated. Dear God in heaven, all the clues had been there. He'd just been too lost in a rosy fog of love and hope to see them.

Given time, that was a problem he could surely overcome. The threat of Caro tumbling into West's bed in the meantime was far more immediate. "He's a debauchee and incapable of fidelity."

She frowned in puzzlement. "I thought he was your friend."

He used to be. "That doesn't mean I'm blind to his faults."

Silas's blood thundered to haul her out of that blackguard West's reach. Not to mention all the other boneheads infesting this room. He retained enough of his previously civilized self to resist the impulse. Just.

Love, it seemed, made beasts of men. How wise he'd been to avoid it all these years.

"You could be useful in my search for a lover, you know." Her tone was thoughtful rather than hostile.

Yes, I can kill every one of the encroaching buggers, until I'm the only man standing.

"I can certainly alert you to the rogues and wastrels." Which meant London's entire male population, except for the newly reformed Lord Stone. He tightened his hold on her trim waist and performed a breathtaking twirl, privately claiming her as his and devil take any fellow with different ideas.

"That's what I mean." Despite his childish acrobatics, she remained disgustingly level-headed. "Ladies are at such a disadvantage when it comes to what a man is really like. We see gentlemen all polished and careful of their manners, when any fool knows that they show their true selves to their friends, away from the artificial light of polite society."

Silas regarded her in horror. "You expect me to pimp you to my friends?"

She blushed again. It was odd—until tonight, he'd never seen her blush. This made twice in the space of half an hour. "No, of course not. But if you think I'm making an unwise choice, I'd like you to tell me."

His gut tightened with self-hatred. Her trust remained, despite tonight's numskullery. Now she invited the wolf to guard the sheepfold. If he retained a shred of honor, he should say no. He used to have some principles, for pity's sake.

"I'll do my best," he said, and knew himself the biggest rogue of all.

She glanced over his shoulder again. "Good. Although despite what you say, I still think West might be my best bet—and he's indicated an interest."

Had he, by God? Silas began to plot a slow and painful demise for a man who had been a lifelong companion. "That doesn't mean much. He pursues anything in petticoats."

Another turn and Silas realized that Caro examined the satanically handsome Lord West with a speculative glint in her fine eyes. "So it wouldn't be difficult to win him as a lover? I'd rather not devote months to the preliminaries. He seems more appealing by the minute."

And Silas realized that in becoming his beloved's conspirator, he signed up for a special place in hell.

CHAPTER TWO

*S*ilas's ordeal began the very next night.

Helena made up a party to attend the opera, a lackluster performance of the 'Barber of Seville,' with a Rosina who sounded like a strangled cat. During the first interval, an eager horde of Helena and Fenella's admirers whisked them away, leaving Caro and Silas alone in the dimly lit box.

Perhaps an opportunity? He moved to the chair beside her at the front. More than once, he'd used an opera box's privacy to promote a flirtation. But Caro turned to him with shining eyes and such a deuced trusting expression on her face that all amorous stratagems turned tail and fled.

She looked lovely in a purple gown of some shiny material that turned her skin to silky cream. And wasn't that a nonsensical bit of description? Since meeting Caro, he'd fallen victim to poetical fatuity.

Damn it, he was a man of science. But nothing in his vials and beakers could compare to her beauty. He had a sick feeling that before he was done, he'd be rhyming June and moon—and calling himself a loon for good measure.

"Silas, I've been thinking about our conversation last night."

So, devil take her, had he. "You've reconsidered taking a lover?"

A faint frown appeared between her brows. "No, of course not."

"Oh," he said glumly.

"This isn't a whim. I've thought long and hard about my plans." It was her turn to sound glum. "The world leaves widows a lot of time to think. I've had more than a year to mull over my intentions."

He'd spent a year mulling over his intentions, too. He'd been planning a journey down the aisle. She'd been planning a progress from one lucky sod's bed to the next. The most galling element was that she seemed ready to consider any fool in London as a potential lover. Except for one Silas Nash.

It was enough to drive a fellow stark, staring mad.

"I don't believe you've thought of the consequences," he said, wishing he could come up with something scary enough to deter her.

Her blue eyes remained steady. "I suppose you mean pregnancy."

He brightened. Yes, that would fit the bill perfectly.

It said something for his distraction that he hadn't immediately mentioned the possibility. "It's a risk." He paused. "Especially after vigorous and prolonged sexual activity."

He'd shoot the scoundrel who invited her to partake of such activity. If anyone was going to talk her into bed, it was him. Then he'd give her vigorous and prolonged until she was dizzy with pleasure. He'd panted after Caro for an eon. He had a lot of energy to burn off.

He'd hoped his plain speaking might discourage her. Of course it didn't. Instead that damnably guileless gaze fastened on his face. "I want a lover worthy of the name. A bit of heat is well overdue."

Good God, her frankness compounded his torment. He shifted on his spindly seat to relieve his discomfort and thanked heaven that the poor light hid his swift physical reaction. A bit of heat? At this rate, the Theatre Royal would go up in flames before Almaviva won the caterwauling Rosina.

"What will you do if you find yourself with child?" How ironic that he, the great debaucher, counseled prudence. Somewhere the angels were laughing their heads off at him.

"I was married for ten years without conceiving." Fleeting sadness dulled her eyes. "The most obvious conclusion is that I'm barren."

Her prosaic tone didn't deceive him. He forgot his schemes and wounded pride, and only remembered that he hated to see her unhappy. He took the slender gloved hand resting on the box's edge. "I'm sorry, Caro."

For a moment, her hand lay in his, and he hoped she might at last confide in him about her marriage. Only after she brought her fears into the light could he vanquish them. But to his regret, she swiftly resumed her social mask and withdrew. The warmth of her touch lingered. For a year, his love had survived on these small crumbs. He felt like he slowly starved to death.

She attempted a smile. "I've been listing candidates."

He straightened in his chair, the need to assuage her heartache battling with his primitive masculine compulsion to see off all competitors. "Oh?"

She nodded with every appearance of confidence, but the hands she twined together betrayed uncertainty. Was that a sign that she wasn't as set on this path as she sounded? He stifled the urge to tell her to give up this tomfoolery and marry him. Last night's quarrel had been a sharp reminder that he could still lose this game.

When he didn't question her sanity the way he had at her ball, she sucked in a relieved breath. "Perhaps you can tell me about them."

With difficulty he kept his expression neutral. "Delighted to help," he said, lying through his teeth.

After a hesitation as if she sensed something amiss

but couldn't place it, she said, "Mr. Harslett has been very attentive, and he has pretty manners."

"Old Johnny Harslett?" Silas asked, playing for time.

"Yes, there he is. The tall gentleman with red hair."

"I know who he is." Silas shot a poisonous glare at the oblivious clodpoll standing in the pit below them.

"Then what do I need to know?"

Hell. Silas had never heard a word against Harslett, something of a miracle in the vicious world they inhabited. Time for a bit of creativity. He lowered his voice to a confidential murmur. "Completely under his mother's thumb. Doesn't have a thought to call his own."

"I'm not expecting him to invite me to tea with his family."

Silas lowered his voice further. "Yes, but his mother insists on...choosing his mistresses. And interviewing them after every...encounter."

She gaped with shock before distaste crossed her features. "Ugh. Very well. I take your point. He's not suitable." She pointed to another section of the crowded ground floor. "What about him?"

"Lord Pascal?"

"He's very handsome."

Devil take the fellow, he was. Amy, Silas's youngest sister, had been moon-eyed over him when she was twelve. These days, at sixteen, she was more interested in efficient farming methods, thank heaven. Silas racked his brains for some reason to veto Pascal as Caro's lover.

"He chews with his mouth open." When that didn't elicit an immediate rejection, he pursued his fiction. "And he cracks his knuckles incessantly. He'd drive you completely dotty within five minutes."

"What about Harry Hall?" She pointed to the slender man talking to Pascal.

"Doesn't wash."

She turned to frown at Silas in puzzlement. "I've danced with him. He smelled perfectly fine."

"Well, when I say he doesn't wash, he does have a scrub-down once a month. You must have timed your dance just right."

"Oh, dear," she said with unconcealed disappointment. "Eligible lovers seem thinner on the ground than I'd anticipated. I'm so glad you're helping me to discount the bad choices."

If he had his way, he'd have her discounting every rake, roué, mother's boy, and decent chap in London. Except for that fine example of British manhood Silas Nash.

She brightened as her eyes settled on a tall, brown-haired man in the opposite box. "There's Lord Garson. You can't tell me he's unsuitable. I know you're great friends."

A friendship likely to end in bloodshed if Caro went to the swine's bed. Silas struggled to come up with something to dissuade her from pursuing a fellow he both liked and respected. His honor dangled by a thread, but he couldn't bring himself to accuse a good man of cheating at cards or swindling old ladies.

Garson caught his eye and signaled a greeting. Then he raised his quizzing glass to inspect Caroline with unconcealed interest. A shamefully primeval itch to poke the delicate implement into Garson's eye gripped Silas.

"He...snores," he said in a strangled voice.

"Is that all? We won't do much sleeping."

Buggeration, now he was imagining her *not sleeping* with Garson. The pictures swarming through his mind made him long to smash his fist into his friend's wholly inoffensive face. "Caro, you shock me."

She looked unimpressed. "No, I don't. Anyway, how do you know?"

"Know what?"

"That he snores."

Silas hadn't lied so much since he was a lad caught raiding Woodley Park larder at midnight. "A few years ago I had the misfortune of sharing a room with him at a dashed poky hunting box in the Cairngorms. Didn't get a wink of sleep. Every breath sounded like a battery of artillery."

"I agree that's a disqualification in a husband, but it's not really a problem in a lover."

The devil, what else could he say against his dear, much admired friend? "And he picks his teeth. It's worse than Pascal's knuckle cracking."

Caro cast him a doubtful glance. "Are you sure? People do nothing but sing his praises, and nobody's mentioned any unfortunate personal habits."

Silas shrugged and strove to look reliable. "I'm only telling you what I know. You were the one who asked me to snitch on my friends. You ought to be grateful that I'm breaking the gentlemen's code for your sake."

"You're right. I'm sorry." A ruminative expression entered her eyes. "From what you've said, West sounds the best of the lot."

Bloody hell. All that lying and Silas was no further advanced than he'd been last night. "He's not right for you."

"I don't see why not. Unless you're going to accuse him of snoring or picking his teeth or crunching his knuckles. I know he washes and his mother is a charming lady. She came to one of Helena's teas." Before he could gather his arguments, she sent him a brilliant smile. "Thank you, Silas. You've been most helpful."

Helpful? Someone should hit him with a hammer before he was so helpful again. As if to underline the stinking morass Silas waded into, West glanced up from the stalls and smiled at Caroline, damn his sneaky, covetous, lecherous, thieving eyes.

And Silas's beloved smiled back with a cordiality that made him want to snarl like an angry mastiff.

～

A soft tap on Silas's bedroom door interrupted disturbed dreams where he chased endlessly after Caro, and she chased endlessly after some faceless man. Round and round, and nobody laying a hand on their quarry. Feeling exhausted with all that running, he cracked open one eye. The room was dark. He groaned and rolled over to bury his face in the pillow. Whoever the hell it was would go away.

Except there was another knock and the faint squeak of an opening door, before a tentative voice asked, "My lord?"

"If you don't get out in the next five seconds, Dobbs, you'll be seeking alternative employment," Silas mumbled without raising his head.

"I'm sorry to hear that, sir," his valet said calmly.

"Five, four, three—"

"Your sister is downstairs and requests your presence."

That was surprising enough for Silas to roll over and stare blearily through the gloom at the cadaverous-looking fellow holding a candle. "It's the middle of the night."

Dobbs's expression didn't change. It never did. "Not quite, sir. Close on six o'clock."

"What the devil is my sister doing here?" He felt thickheaded. It wasn't altogether lack of sleep. Last night when the prospect of Caro tumbling into West's arms had become unendurable, he'd sought refuge in the brandy bottle. The pincers behind his eyes reminded him why he so rarely indulged.

"Lady Crewe is dressed for riding."

Of course she was. His favorite sister was mad for the horses. Or she had been his favorite, before she started barging in on a chap when any sensible person would still be in bed.

Dobbs placed the candle on a chest of drawers and crossed to open the curtains. The pale morning light made Silas wince.

"Shall I help you dress before you go downstairs, my lord?" Dobbs lifted Silas's velvet dressing gown from the chair where he'd flung it last night.

Silas forced himself to sit up. Each movement felt like pushing a boulder up a steep hill. "No, the dressing gown will suffice. There might be an emergency."

"Lady Crewe didn't appear agitated."

That didn't mean much. Helena could keep her head up through a hurricane. God knew, she'd needed all her pride and courage when she'd lived with Crewe.

Silas grunted acknowledgment as he let Dobbs slide the heavy crimson robe over his bare shoulders. "I'm awake now, Dobbs. You can go back to bed."

"Thank you, sir, but in case Lady Crewe's tidings require further action, I might wait. In the meantime, I'll make some coffee."

"Bless you." Silas strode toward the door. "I mightn't sack you today after all."

Dobbs didn't smile. "Most appreciated, sir."

Silas rushed downstairs and slammed into the drawing room. The family had an extravagant townhouse in Berkeley Square, but he preferred to rent rooms here in Albemarle Street where he could preserve a little privacy. Although if his sister planned to stage more midnight invasions, privacy might be a thing of the past.

"Helena, what the hell are you doing here?"

"And good morning to you, too, brother." She stood near the unlit hearth, tall, striking, stylish in her close-fitting black habit. Apart from the commanding Nash nose they shared, nobody would ever pick them for brother and sister.

Silas dredged up a smile and sauntered across to kiss her on the cheek. "Is there some emergency?"

She sank gracefully onto the sofa beside the mantel. "You might think there is."

He frowned. His sisters occasionally involved him in small dramas, but he couldn't recall anything worthy of a predawn visit. "Is all well with the family?"

"As far as I know." Helena set her riding crop on her lap and stared hard at him. "I've come to invite you to ride in Hyde Park."

"What drivel is this?"

Grim humor twisted his sister's lips. "Perhaps it is drivel, but I'm joining Caro in an hour."

"I don't—" he began, increasingly irritated, but Helena interrupted him.

"With Lord West."

"Hell's bells," he muttered, hands fisting at his sides as he prepared to thump his absent rival. When he raised his eyes, he read knowledge in Helena's expression. "You know."

She shrugged. "That you're head over heels in love with Caro? Of course I do."

He hated to think that he'd been so transparent—and that she might find his lack of success amusing. Helena's sense of humor tended toward the black. "How?"

"Because I know you, dear Silas. I've never seen you so careful with a woman. It's rather touching."

His lips tightened. "You mock me."

She shook her dark head, topped with a high-crowned beaver hat tied with a fluttering violet scarf. "Not at all. I've always known you had a capacity for deep feeling—you show it to the family, but not to the rest of the world. Nice to see you're not nearly as self-sufficient as people paint you. I guessed something serious was on the cards when no lady's name has been linked to yours in more than a year. I fear you've become that mythical beast, a reformed rake."

He winced. "How dull."

Her laugh held the familiar wry note. "No. You're growing up at last."

What in Satan's name did one say to that? Fortunately Dobbs arrived with the promised coffee and saved him from replying. Silas snatched a cup and emptied it in a gulp, his brain at last starting to function.

"She doesn't know I love her," Silas said when Dobbs had left.

"No." Helena lifted her red and gold cup from the table beside her and took a more decorous sip than he'd managed. "Despite ten years of marriage, Caro's an innocent. She was so young when she was wed, and Freddie Beaumont never recognized her potential to be anything more than a rural wife. She's clever, but she's inexperienced in the wiles of wicked fellows like you. For all her wit and beauty, she's a wide-eyed child in many ways."

"I want her to stay that way," Silas said grimly. He refilled his cup and strolled across to stand beside the sofa. "She won't if she falls into West's clutches."

Helena regarded him with disfavor. "He's no worse than you."

"He'll hurt her."

Helena shrugged again. "Perhaps. Perhaps not. She's not in love with him. It's love that hurts, after all."

Silas forgot his romantic troubles long enough to lay one hand on his sister's slender shoulder. "I wish I'd shot that bastard Crewe."

"If anyone should have shot him, it was me. But let's not spoil our morning with talk of that brute."

His sister never spoke of the hell of her marriage. Silas suspected revisiting those dark years gave her late, unlamented spouse power over her present. The problem was that the poison continued to taint her view of the world. He compared the wild hoyden she'd been as a girl with this contained, sardonic woman, and his heart cramped with grief for her. "You could have sent me a note last night."

She surveyed him thoughtfully over her coffee. "I hadn't decided to interfere then. I'm still not sure I should."

It was his turn to look at his sister with disfavor. "Why in Hades not? She'll make me a fine wife."

"Undoubtedly. I'm sure she made Freddie Beaumont a fine wife, too. Not one to shirk her duty, our Caro. I think that's one of the reasons she doesn't want to sign up for more of the same."

Pique stirred. "I would hope marriage to me would involve more than duty."

"It would involve a commitment, when she's only now tasting her first freedom."

"I have no intention of crushing her spirit."

"Maybe not. But she'd be a wife, when I know she's looking forward to an eventful widowhood."

"With that ruffian West," he said grumpily.

"And who knows who else?"

"Bloody hell," Silas said, setting his cup down in its saucer with a sharp clink. "It's enough to make a man want to shoot himself."

Helena laughed briefly. "Not when I've taken this trouble to alert you to your lady love's latest escapade.

Why don't you get dressed, and we'll see what's happening in the park?"

"Capital idea." Silas strode toward the door. "And, Helena, thank you."

Caroline drew her roan mare to a halt beneath the oak tree where she'd arranged to meet Helena and Lord West. She hadn't been up this early since she'd put aside her mourning, but she'd stayed home last night after West had suggested she join him on his morning ride. Despite Silas's warnings, she found herself increasingly pleased with her choice of lover. So far, thank heaven, West showed every sign of reciprocating her interest.

When she heard hoof beats, she turned to watch West cantering toward her on a magnificent bay. He was tall and lean and sat his horse like a king. Admiration filled her. He truly was a sight to behold, especially for a woman starting to sample the banquet life offered a presentable widow with an impressive fortune. She had an invigorating sense that her new life stretched before her along a broad, bright path.

As he approached, he swept his hat from his ruffled ebony curls and bowed. "My Lady Beaumont, good morning."

She smiled, wondering why her heart didn't dip the way it had when she'd seen Silas at her ball—before he began acting like an ass. "Good morning, my lord. It looks like fine weather."

"It does indeed."

Platitudes. But then she and West weren't far from strangers. Of course, she'd heard the gossip about his sins. As she'd told Silas, his reputation was no deterrent. She wanted a proficient lover to show her what she'd missed in Freddie's infrequent embrace. She didn't want or expect deep affection.

And she needed to stop thinking about Silas.

Which proved difficult when she turned to speak to her groom and she saw Helena, invited, and Silas, uninvited, as least by her, trotting in her direction. Early morning sun through the fresh green foliage lit them like characters in a play. Silas was laughing at something Helena said, his face creased in swift amusement.

That silly little tremor in her heart was back. How very odd.

West's classically handsome face showed no whit of disappointment at Silas's presence. But then of course, a brother and sister riding together was nothing notable, and Caroline's friendship with the family was well known. "She sits a horse like an Amazon," he murmured.

Helena did indeed look at home on her big black gelding. "This is the first time I've seen her on horseback."

"You should see her ride with the local hunt up in

Leicestershire. A genteel trot around Hyde Park can't convey her magnificence. She takes your breath away."

Caroline regarded him curiously. "I forgot that your estates aren't far from the Nashes'."

He turned to her and suddenly she found him more appealing than ever before. The rueful smile in his deep-set green eyes changed him from a hero in a novel to someone much warmer and more approachable. "We grew up together. Helena used to try to boss me around."

Caroline laughed. "She always thinks she knows best, doesn't she? The problem is that she usually does."

"Good morning, West, Caro." The faint chill in Silas's voice made Caroline's head snap up. Was she still out of favor? She'd hoped their recent awkwardness had passed. Three nights ago at the opera, he'd seemed his usual self. Well, mostly. Upon reflection, she'd wondered how truthful he'd been about his friends. Especially when he'd made no secret of his dislike of her plans.

"Good morning," Helena said, and Caroline caught the critical glance she cast her brother. "Silas decided to join us. I hope you don't mind."

"I was telling Lady Beaumont that I pulled your pigtails when you were an infant."

Helena's unreadable dark gaze settled on West. "Yes, you were an abominable child."

His eyes glittered bright emerald. "You didn't

always think that, Helena. I gave you your first kiss, if I recall."

Surprised, Caroline studied her friend. Helena hadn't confided that particular morsel. "Helena, you must tell me more."

If West's announcement embarrassed Helena, she didn't show it. The haughty features beneath the stylish hat remained impassive. "In truth, I'd forgotten. How kind of you to remind me, West. I wouldn't expect you to remember. After all, you've had so many...kisses since."

Caroline caught West's chagrin, but it was gone before she could interpret it. "You unsheathe your claws early in the day, Lady Crewe," he said neutrally, although something told Caroline that his reaction was anything but neutral. It seemed that Helena and West shared a long history. Not altogether a happy one either.

"You two can't help yourselves," Silas said lightly from the back of his dapple gray. "You're giving Caro quite the wrong impression of our childhood revels. Shall we ride?"

Caroline had hoped to use this meeting to further her acquaintance with West, but conscience made her rein in beside Helena while the two men went ahead. "Are you all right?"

Helena turned an opaque dark gaze upon her. She hardly seemed aware of the need to control the huge brute of a horse ambling along the path in perfect docility. West was right. She was clearly an adept horsewoman. "I'd dearly love a good long gallop. Curse the dictates of propriety."

Her friend's evasion didn't distract Caroline. "I had no idea you and West were so close."

Helena's eyes narrowed on West's back in its superbly cut black coat. "We're not."

"It sounds like you are. Or at least you were."

She shrugged. "We've always rubbed each other up the wrong way."

Caroline bit her lip, unsure whether to speak her mind. Helena could be prickly when someone peered beneath her unconcerned manner to the painful secrets beneath. But this was important. "If you have your eye on West, I can step aside."

A mocking smile curled Helena's lips. "That's astonishingly generous."

"You're my friend."

"In love and war, no rules apply."

Caroline frowned, wishing she didn't have to devote quite so much of her attention to steering her horse. She was only a middling rider while it was obvious that West and the Nash siblings were crackers in the saddle. "As you know, this is neither. I'm certainly not in love with West, and he's not in love with me. Nor is there any war."

Helena cast her an enigmatic glance. "I wouldn't be too sure about that." Before Caroline could question the odd statement, she went on. "I'm not convinced

West is the answer to your prayers."

"Because you want him for yourself?"

Helena's clear laugh rang out, causing the two gentlemen to glance back. "Good God, no. I've had more than my fill of coxcombs."

West scowled at her, apparently guessing that her unguarded remark referred to him. He kicked his horse into a canter and drew ahead of the party.

"That wasn't kind," Caroline said quietly.

"No, but it was accurate," Helena muttered.

"Is he a coxcomb? I grant that you know him better than I do, but his manners are delightful, he's intelligent, and I'd lay half my fortune he knows what to do with a woman."

"Caro, spare my blushes."

"Behave yourself. You know exactly why I'm interested in West. I want some passing entertainment—if even half the talk is true, he's the man to give it to me."

The amusement drained from Helena's face. "I don't want you hurt."

Caroline regarded Helena with displeasure. "You're as bad as your brother." Which reminded her of another reason to rebuke her friend. "What on earth made you invite Silas along this morning?"

"He enjoys riding."

"Not at the crack of dawn."

"You do him an injustice. He's often in his greenhouses early."

"Yes, well, that's different and you know it."

"You're usually delighted to see him. Is there trouble in paradise? What happened at your ball? For a few minutes there, you looked ready to murder him."

Broodingly Caroline studied Silas's straight back as he rode ahead. For over a year, he'd been a dear friend. Something at her ball had changed the balance between them, even before he'd come over so highhanded and judgmental. And although they hadn't kept the quarrel going at the opera, something had been wrong.

She resisted revisiting those unsettling seconds when she'd looked at him and her heart skipped a beat or two. Of course he was attractive. She'd always recognized that. But she didn't want a short affair with Silas, and right now, a short affair was all she was after. Assuming she could persuade him to see her as more than an honorary sister.

"Caro?" Helena probed when the silence extended.

"He doesn't approve of my plans to bed West. Not that it's any of his concern."

"He cares about you."

"I care about him, too, but I wouldn't dream of telling him to stay away from opera dancers and high-flying widows."

Helena smiled. "You promise to become a high-flier yourself. What did you call us? The dashing widows?"

Caroline made herself return the smile. "A dashing widow goes after what she wants. Which means, my dear Helena, that I intend to ignore your brother's censure."

"Was it as bad as that?"

"It was." Caroline's lips firmed with annoyance. What right had Silas to lay down the law? If she wanted a tyrant running her life, she'd damn well marry again. "And dashing widows don't hang back gossiping with their friends when they've been bold enough to arrange a rendezvous with a lover."

"West isn't your lover."

"Not yet. But despite what Silas says, I think he could very well be. When I listed my requirements in a paramour, I could have been describing West."

"Good God, Caro, taking a lover isn't like shopping for a new bonnet."

"Isn't it?" Caroline studied West. Silas had caught up with him and was managing a civil conversation despite his dire warnings to her. "So far, I'd say it's exactly like that. The latest fashion? Yes. Becoming to wear in public? Yes. Likely to raise the envy of other ladies? Yes. Comfortable to put on? Yes."

"If you say just the right size, you really will make me blush," Helena said on a gurgle of laughter.

Caroline was the one who blushed. "In truth, I'm woefully out of the way of judging a man's prowess. I was barely out of the schoolroom when I married Freddie, and he was never the most passionate of husbands. Not to mention he was ill for the last three years of his life."

Helena's eyes softened. "You feel you've missed out on something."

Caroline's smile was cocky. "I know I have."

"West is the man to supply the lack?"

"I sincerely hope so. Let's hope he finds me equally appealing. After all, I'm not nearly as sophisticated as the women he's used to."

Helena's gaze was searching. "You're a diamond compared to the hussies he usually pursues. He'd be a fool not to follow up on your overtures."

"Thank you." Caroline reached across to squeeze one of Helena's gloved hands, lying loosely on the reins and keeping the behemoth of a horse as mellow as a sleepy lapdog. "I just need to keep my nerve. I've spent far too long waiting for life to happen to me. It's time I took control of my destiny."

Helena didn't smile back. "And that destiny is Vernon Grange, Baron West?"

"For a month or two, anyway," she said casually.

Unwilling to answer any more questions or to reveal that her worldly attitude was totally manufactured, Caroline urged her mare forward until she rode beside the man she set out to seduce.

CHAPTER THREE

*A*t the Oldhams' ball, Caroline waltzed with Lord West. She should be pleased with how their acquaintance had progressed in the fortnight since their ride in Hyde Park. At the events they attended, he always made a point of singling her out for a conversation and danced with her twice—more often would set tongues wagging. That pleased her, too. She might intend to take a lover, but she wanted to be discreet about it.

The Oldhams had hired the same orchestra that Caroline had imported for her ball, which as she had hoped was the year's most talked-about event. Unfortunately the lilting music might as well have been a band of rusty shovels banging together, for all the attention she paid it.

"Lady Beaumont, you seem distracted. Would you

like to sit down and I'll fetch you a glass of champagne?" West asked.

She stared up into his handsome face and told herself she should relish being his chosen partner. She'd intercepted enough envious glances from the other ladies to know he'd have no trouble replacing her.

Perhaps that was the problem. He danced with her because she was an acclaimed success. She danced with him because he matched the cardboard cutout lover she'd created in her mind during her lonely year of mourning. For all their mutual amity, neither felt a scrap of genuine affinity. Dancing in his arms was, frankly, less thrilling than holding Silas's hand at the opera the other night.

She bolstered failing resolution. Once she'd given herself to West, these corrosive doubts would disappear. It was natural that she hesitated on the brink of action. She'd only ever slept with one man. If she could bring herself to seduce West, she'd finally escape the prison of her past. But if she lost her nerve now, she feared she'd never find the courage to lead the daring, exciting life she'd always longed for.

"Lady Beaumont?"

She must be gaping at him like a moonling. At this rate, he'd seek more amusing company. And she'd know her brave claim to be a dashing widow was nothing more than hot air. She couldn't bear to revert to the subdued, provincial woman who had arrived in

London more than a year ago. She raised her chin and met his eyes. One thing at least needed to change. No red-blooded rake bedded a woman he called Lady Beaumont.

"My lord, we've gone beyond formalities. Please call me Caroline."

His startled reaction was discouraging—and unexpected. Perhaps he wasn't as awake to her naughty intentions as she imagined. "I'd be honored."

She waited for him to extend the same courtesy, but instead he began to outline his plans for the rest of the week. Caroline berated herself for drifting off again. After all, he was ensuring that they'd meet. That confirmed his interest. She reminded herself that any woman would be proud to call this man her lover.

Whatever Silas thought of her plans.

Silas who had avoided her since that ride in Hyde Park. Helena said he was busy with his botanical work, but Caroline had seen him out in society every night. He hadn't lacked for dance partners—even if none had been his dear friend, Lady Beaumont.

On the rare occasions they'd spoken, he greeted her with a chill politeness that hurt, however much she pretended it didn't. She supposed he was sulking because she refused to heed his misgivings about her plans. She'd tried to tease him out of his mood. After all, they'd always made each other laugh. But any attempts to re-establish their closeness foundered against that wall of politeness, cold and impassable as the Atlantic.

As if the thought conjured him up, she glimpsed him across the crowded room. He was dancing with Fenella who looked lovely in a rose pink gown. Considering how reluctantly Fen had abandoned her widow's weeds, she'd taken to the season with an élan that astonished Caroline.

Now there she was, sparkling and pretty and happy, in Silas's arms. He smiled down at her with the warmth he'd once reserved for Caroline.

They looked so right together. Somehow complete unto one another.

Like people in love.

A great ax of understanding slammed down from nowhere and smashed everything Caroline thought she knew into chaos. The couples whirling around her became a dizzying wall of color. On a muffled cry, she stumbled as West swept her into a turn.

"Lady Beaumont—Caroline—you're not well." West's hand firmed around her waist. "Come. Sit down."

"I'm...I'm fine." Her voice came from far away as she clung to West's powerful arm.

"You're definitely not fine," he said, and somewhere in the distant reaches of her mind, she registered his kindness. "Can you walk or should I carry you?"

"No, no, I can walk," she forced out. Talking was

painful. Her heart shrank to the size of a walnut, and the breath jammed in her closed throat.

Hardly aware of moving, she let him lead her across to where Helena stood surrounded by a circle of admirers. Vaguely Caroline knew that heads turned to track her unsteady progress.

"Helena, Lady Beaumont is feeling faint," West said, his arm still around her waist.

She was grateful for his support. Her legs threatened to fold beneath her. She told herself to stand up straight, but every muscle felt made of string.

"Caro, are you ill?" Helena asked, taking her arm. "Here. Sit down. It's cursed hot in here. No wonder you're lightheaded."

"I'll fetch some water," West said.

"Thank you," Helena said, easing Caroline down into a chair. She waved the curious onlookers away. "Stand clear and give her some space."

As her blood thundered deafeningly in her ears, Caroline sucked in a deep breath of humid air, then another. It didn't help. The musicians scratching away at the far end of the room set her teeth on edge.

Horrified at her behavior, she summoned the stern voice in her head that always sounded like her father at his frostiest. That austere voice told her she made a spectacle of herself. Over nothing. Less than nothing.

Silas. And Fenella.

West returned, looking gratifyingly perturbed, but she was in no state to enjoy his attention. With a shaky hand, she accepted the glass he carried. How desperately she wished she was at home, away from all these prying eyes.

She choked down a sip of water, then forced numb lips to move. Her apology emerged slurred and muffled. "I'm sorry for all this fuss. I'm fine. Really."

"You're as pale as a ghost," Helena said, fanning her.

"What the devil's going on?" Silas pushed his way through the small crowd. "Has something happened to Caro?"

"Lady Beaumont felt faint," West said.

"Caro, are you all right?" Fenella rushed up behind Silas. She sounded sincerely worried. Of course she did. Fen was an angel, one of the kindest people in the world.

Silas. And Fenella .

"I just need a moment," Caroline whispered. She forced down another sip, her mind seething as she struggled to make sense of what she'd seen and, more, why it stabbed at her like a knife. How could she have been so blind? Now that she saw, why, in the name of all that was holy, was she so upset? She'd long ago recognized that she lacked Fen's generous spirit, but she thought she was better than this. Or was she at heart one of those ghastly women who hated to see a friend find new allegiances, new love? She couldn't bear to admit she was such a spiteful cat.

Yet still those three words jammed like logs in her chest. *Silas. And Fenella.*

"Caro, tell me what's wrong," Silas said, seizing her hand. "Do you need a doctor?"

She snatched away and refused to meet his eyes. If Silas picked up even a hint of why she was so distraught, she'd die of humiliation.

"No, I'm fine." If she kept saying it, perhaps it would become true.

"You don't look any better," Helena said.

"Let me take you home," Silas said gently. He sounded like the man who had been her friend, and that only magnified her roiling misery. "The heat in here is unbearable."

"I'll come with you, Caro." Fenella watched her with such aching concern that Caroline felt like a witch for wanting to claw that sweet face to ribbons. "I'm visiting Brandon at Eton tomorrow which means an early start."

What business of hers was it if Silas flirted with Fenella? Except she'd read more than passing attraction in his face. She'd read a closeness that made her feel bereft and lonely. She'd seen abiding affection and deep interest.

Dear God, she really was a shrew. Despite her pursuit of West, she wanted Silas's affection and interest all to herself.

"No need to interrupt your enjoyment." She prayed she didn't sound as waspish to them as she did in her own ears.

"Nonsense." Through the buzzing in Caroline's

head, she heard an unaccustomed note of authority in Fenella's voice. Of course, the love of a man like Silas Nash would do wonders for any woman's confidence.

Caroline's protests came to naught. She ended up in Silas's carriage, sitting opposite him and beside Fenella. She'd regained a little of her composure, but everything still felt vilely disjointed. No amount of self-castigation could silence the howling protest deep in her soul at the idea of Silas and Fenella in love.

To avoid questions she flinched from answering, she closed her eyes and huddled in the corner. On the short journey, Silas and Fenella spoke in low voices. It didn't help Caroline's raging, unacceptable, uncontrollable jealousy that their discussion centered on her welfare. Not even her nastiest suspicions detected anything but fondness in their remarks.

Silas. And Fenella.

It made such cruelly good sense. Fenella would appeal to Silas's innate protective streak, the same protective streak that had led him to befriend a lonely widow from soggiest Lincolnshire. Fenella, like Silas, would face down lions for the sake of someone she loved. When she'd first met Fenella, Caroline had dismissed her as a clinging vine. But she'd come to respect her friend's loyalty to her dead husband and her fierce devotion to her son. Fenella mightn't look like a warrior, but that didn't mean she couldn't fight.

What a pity that at this moment, Caroline wanted to shove her into a bottomless well.

If Silas pursued Fenella, it was likely that he had marriage in mind. And why shouldn't he? Fenella would make the ideal wife—and unlike Caroline, she'd proven herself capable of bearing children.

That old, bitter failure stuck its claws into her anew. The prospect of Silas and Fenella producing a brood of perfect offspring made her feel like vomiting. Under cover of the darkness, she pressed a shaking hand to her churning stomach. She didn't want to be the sort of woman who turned sick with jealousy. But apparently she was.

All the time, her conscience remonstrated with her that she should be happy for her friends, that she pursued Lord West, that people had a perfect right to set up alliances separate from Caroline Beaumont and her selfish whims.

She'd like to drown her conscience in that well, too.

Caroline only emerged from self-torture when the luxurious carriage drew to a stop and the door opened. She'd been too lost in her funk to realize they'd reached her house. She fumbled for her reticule and shawl as Fenella stepped out.

Oh, for pity's sake, no. She couldn't bear it. If that hussy—who also happened to be a dear friend—planned to stay behind to ensure her wellbeing, she'd scream like a banshee.

"Good night, Caro. I'll come and see how you are when I get back from Eton."

Caroline frowned through the gloom, one hand

clutching her reticule, the other fisted in her cashmere shawl. Then she glanced over her friend's shoulder to the footman holding the door at the top of the steps. Fenella's, not hers.

"This is your house," she said stupidly.

"Silas will take you the rest of the way. It's only a few minutes—I doubt if even the highest sticklers would find that improper. I hope you don't mind."

"No," Caroline said, meaning she'd rather cut off her head than suffer a private conversation with Silas Nash. Silas who would press for answers and who was smart enough to read between the lines to discern what a hag she was.

But Fenella took that croaked denial as consent. "Go straight to bed when you get home. Conquering society has overstretched you."

She leaned in to kiss Caroline's cheek. The brush of her lips burned like acid. Oh, Caroline Beaumont was a horrid person. She was the one who should be dunked in that well.

"Good night," she mumbled, shrinking back into the unlit cabin and refusing to watch as Silas escorted Fenella inside. He was hardly likely to kiss her in public. Which didn't stop Caroline imagining them falling into a passionate embrace the minute they crossed the threshold.

If Silas did kiss Fenella—even in her half-mad state, Caroline knew that was extremely unlikely—he didn't take long about it. He was soon back in the carriage.

As they rolled on, she felt Silas studying her through the darkness. He had his back to the horses while she faced forward. She suffered an illogical, pathetic impulse to ask him to sit beside her and take her into his arms. She'd never felt so alone in her life.

"I'm sorry to interrupt your delightful evening." This time, not even the kindest ear could miss the sour note.

"Are you feeling better?" he said mildly. "You looked ready to collapse at the Oldhams'."

"How considerate of you to notice."

His sigh was long-suffering. "What's wrong, Caro? You've been staring daggers at me all week."

I want you to be my friend again. I want you to smile at me the way you used to. I want to know that you and I are united in a conspiracy against the rest of the world. I want you to tell me that you're not in love with Fenella.

Of course she didn't say any of that. It would be too revealing.

"There's nothing wrong," she muttered, looking blindly out at the rows of quiet houses along South Audley Street.

She didn't need to see his frown to know it was there. "Perhaps you should get out of London for a few days. Fenella's right. You've thrown yourself into the season like a general on campaign. It's time to rest on your laurels before the next battle." His tone hardened. "West will wait a week or so, I'm sure."

The jibe hurt. What right had Silas to point the

finger of disapproval? Temper came to her rescue. She'd rather be angry than bawl like a lost calf. She faced him, catching the glint of his eyes through the darkness. "I could take him with me."

Except strangely, Vernon Grange wasn't her preferred companion in this mythical rural idyll. The man she wanted to be alone with was Silas Nash. She must be losing her mind.

"Why don't you?" Silas asked with a bite. He reached out to grip the base of the open window. The light from the carriage's exterior lamps shone on fingers curled taut over the dark wood. "I'm sure he'd leap at the chance to consummate your affair in some secret love nest."

His contemptuous tone made her bristle. "Who's to say the consummation hasn't already taken place?" she asked with poisonous sweetness.

His breath hissed out before a lacerating silence crashed down. Caroline's stomach knotted in horror. What the devil was wrong with her? Frantically she wished the lying words unsaid, but pride stopped her from backtracking.

After what felt like an hour, Silas spoke. She braced for another lecture on her recklessness, but he sounded tired and flat in a way she'd never heard him before. "I hope you'll both be very happy."

"We are," she said defiantly, even as she told herself it was time to shut up. In fact, she should have kept her mouth closed the entire trip.

"Then I'm bloody delighted for you," he said savagely.

The coach stopped outside her house. Caroline had never imagined she'd be so desperate to escape Silas. In earlier, happier days, the time they spent together had always seemed too short, they had so much to say. She'd lost him, and she didn't know why. The skin across her temples was tight and throbbing with a headache. She longed for the privacy to cry her eyes out in a way she hadn't since she was a silly girl.

"Good night, Silas," she said in a thick voice, her hand fumbling for the catch on the door. She didn't want to spend a moment longer in this carriage than she had to.

"Caro, wait," he said softly, catching her arm just as she found the trick of the fastening.

"I'm tired," she said, hating the whine in her voice. No wonder Silas preferred Fenella.

"I know you are. I've acted like an utter swine. I have no business criticizing your choices. I'm sorry."

Strangely his concession didn't lift her spirits. She was the one who had acted badly, not Silas. "You—"

John, her footman, opened the door and saved her from having to respond to Silas's unnecessary apology. She felt horrible—lumpen and ungracious and stupid and mean. She hadn't felt so useless since she'd forsaken Lincolnshire in search of a reinvented self.

"I'll walk you to your door."

"There's no need," she mumbled.

"You're not well."

"I'm perfectly fine," she said, wondering if they'd carve that lying little phrase on her tombstone.

"Nevertheless."

He wouldn't abandon her until he'd seen her safe, despite the household full of servants awaiting her bidding. Silas was such a white knight. Caroline should have long ago realized that he'd choose a fragile damsel like Fenella, not a great, argumentative, gallumping creature like Caroline Beaumont.

She was too tired and disheartened to insist further. Once he'd escorted her inside, she could send him home. Silently, she left the coach and let him take her arm to help her up the steps. His touch was poignantly tender. He clearly hadn't forgotten her strange turn at the Oldhams'. She wondered what he'd say if she confessed that the sight of him dancing with Fenella had literally made her sick.

"Shall I stay until you're settled?" he asked softly in the doorway after she'd told the footman to wait inside. "I'm not convinced I shouldn't fetch a doctor."

Not long ago, he'd been angry. She didn't sense any anger now. Instead he seemed...sad. That wasn't an adjective she'd ever thought to apply to him. She recalled with stinging regret how his essentially joyous heart had helped her come to terms with her new life.

A joyous heart he'd obviously decided to give to Fenella.

She bit her lip, using the sting to control her tears.

"No," she forced out, then belatedly remembered her manners. "Thank you for bringing me home."

He studied her, the light from inside her house casting fascinating shadows over his face. Then he caught her hand and bowed over it. "You mightn't believe me, but I've only ever wished you well."

"I believe it," she said on a thread of sound. "You're acting like this is goodbye."

Keeping hold of her hand, he watched her from under those expressive brows. "You've learned to fly, Caro. It's inevitable that while you take to the skies, you leave some of us behind on the ground."

She guessed he meant that as a compliment, but it didn't sound like it. It still sounded like farewell, and she could hardly endure the pain of it. "Silas—"

"Good night, Caro. I hope West knows what a damned lucky devil he is."

For the first time, he took the courtly gesture a step further and pressed his lips to her gloved knuckles. Heat jolted her, while unfamiliar yearning jammed her voice in her chest along with her cramping heart.

Abruptly he released her and ran down the steps to his carriage. As the vehicle rumbled across the cobblestones and out of view, she stood on her doorstep, staring after him until she shivered with the cold.

CHAPTER FOUR

Caroline lay in her beautiful mahogany bed—a bed she'd never shared with Freddie, he hadn't brought her to London—and stared dry-eyed into the thick darkness. She felt restless and jumpy and achy.

She'd craved for the relief of tears, but by the time she sent her maid away, her misery had calcified into a hard, painful monolith inside her. So she remained awake, revisiting the night's events and loathing herself. And thinking over her time in London and before that, the barren years of Freddie's illness. Back further to the unhappy young wife—bored, unfulfilled, smothered by an isolation that crushed every drop of life out of her.

It wasn't a very impressive history.

She wasn't a very impressive person.

But until now, at least she'd prided herself on her

sharp wits. When it turned out she was the greatest fool in London. In England. In the world.

With a groan, she turned over to bury her hot face in the cool linen of her pillow. Tonight had battered her with the devastating truth that she'd struggled so hard against acknowledging. Three simple words tortured her. Not the three that had haunted her since she'd looked across a crowded ballroom. *Silas. And Fenella.*

That was bad enough. But worse by far were the three now tormenting her.

I love Silas.

Of course she did. She'd loved him for months. Perhaps from the moment he'd smiled at her across his sister's drawing room and said something teasing to Helena about her ability with calculus contrasting with her ineptitude with tea. Caroline had laughed—he'd made her laugh so often since. She loved his generous spirit. She loved his perceptive, acute mind. She loved his curiosity and his humor.

She loved his quirky, expressive face, and his hazel eyes bright with private amusement. She loved his tall, loose-limbed body with its broad shoulders and narrow hips and strong swordsman's thighs. She loved his competent, powerful hands and his firm, smiling mouth.

She wanted Silas Nash in her bed. She wanted him to press her deep into the mattress as he thrust inside her.

Panting, she rolled onto her back and slid her hand down her belly to her mound. It didn't help. Her touch couldn't answer this desire. Only Silas could do that.

At last the tears broke, trickling down her temples to the pillow. Everything was such a blasted mess. Her love for Silas didn't change the path she followed. After a lifetime of pandering to other people, she refused to surrender her newly acquired freedom.

Not even for love's sake.

Just thinking about her life with Freddie slung crushing chains of fear around her chest. She gasped for air, staring up at the ceiling and telling herself she was free.

Surely there was no need to be so frightened. As long as she didn't yield to this unacceptable love, she'd remain free. She'd sworn on Freddie's early grave that she'd never marry again. Her marriage had been a ten year prison sentence, and while she was sorry Freddie was dead, her strongest and utterly shameful reaction at his passing had been overwhelming relief. Both that Freddie's sufferings were over and that she was no longer obliged to serve him.

Even if Silas wanted her, she couldn't marry him. Not if she meant to be true to herself as she'd never had the chance to be true to herself before. She'd spent every moment of her life under either her father or Freddie's control. Like a fox in a poacher's trap, her soul had strained against that subjugation. These last months, she'd tasted the ambrosia of ordering her own life. The prospect of yielding that independence to a man, no matter how benevolent, made those chains around her chest tighten to the point of agony. Love was just another cage.

That meant if she wanted Silas, she must join the endless parade of his paramours. How long would she hold his attention? A week? A month? Even a year, unprecedented for him, would leave her devastated once it was over. What freedom was there in that?

The stark fact remained. She needed a lover, not someone she loved.

Anyway, if she was right, Silas wasn't remotely interested in Caroline Beaumont. He was in thrall to sweet, charming, delicate Fenella. Even someone as jaded about marriage as Caroline could see how well they suited each other.

She winnowed her memories from the Oldhams' ball for some indication that she was wrong about Silas and Fenella. Perhaps she'd overreacted, although it was hard to argue with Silas and Fen's compatibility. But say he didn't marry Fenella, he'd marry someone. Someone capable of giving him the wholehearted devotion that Caroline couldn't risk because it meant accepting fresh captivity.

Silas wasn't for her, no matter how her stupid heart keened after him.

Far better to enjoy a short, civilized liaison with a sophisticated man who offered pleasure without emotional involvement. West couldn't hurt her because she could never love him. He was perfect.

Even if right now, the thought of handsome Lord West's hands on her body made her stomach heave.

But first she had to make things right with Silas. She owed him an apology for acting like a harpy. Then she owed him her friendship. The excruciating truth was that unless she retreated to the country, she was doomed to see him again and again. He was her best friend's brother. He courted—oh, wicked agony—another close friend.

But tonight, tonight with her love so fresh and so sharp, she'd give herself over to the luxury of imagining Silas Nash in her bed. She'd forget about the shackles of possession and commitment and obedience, and think only of the pleasure her rebellious soul denied her.

Tonight she'd pretend, then she'd put all such dangerous illusions away forever.

With a tremulous sigh, she tugged up the hem of her nightgown and raised her knees. Her hand slipped between her legs, seeking the slick, secret flesh.

Tracking Silas down proved more difficult than Caroline had expected. The day after the Oldhams' ball, he left for Edinburgh to lecture on his experiments. From there, he went to Paris for meetings at the Sorbonne.

When he returned, he retreated to his estates in Leicestershire. Fenella didn't look particularly cast down by his absence, but Caroline wasn't hypocrite enough to encourage confidences about her friend's well-traveled beau.

The season capered toward its end. Caroline made a gallant effort to garner the same enjoyment from the endless round of social events as she had at the beginning. But without Silas, the excitement had gone.

She kept up the pretense that she pursued Lord West, but she doubted even he was convinced of her interest. In all these weeks, they hadn't moved beyond some harmless flirtation and a few dances. She told herself the best cure for pining after Silas was another man's attention. But she couldn't make herself take that last step toward seducing West. And so far, he'd done nothing to deepen their intimacy.

She was surprised that Silas had spoken so slightingly of the man. He was good company, and the admiration in his eyes staved off self-pity.

Yes, she liked Lord West, but he would never set her heart cartwheeling. Only one man did that. And she'd give away every penny of her impressive fortune to change that unwelcome fact.

"Damn it all to hell."

Silas snatched up his latest spindly hybrid and

consigned it to the incinerator heating his greenhouse. Although he didn't live in the Nash townhouse with Helena and his Great Aunt Agnes, he'd built a laboratory in the back garden. Last year, everything he'd touched had turned to gold. He'd started to plan putting a new variety of cherry combining yield, hardiness and sweetness on the market within five years. But all his experiments in recent months had slammed into a wall. He might as well have gone rambling in the Lake District as waste his time poring over seeds and grafts and cuttings.

He'd worked in botany long enough to understand that a man went wrong more often than he went right. Patience was as necessary as soil and water and light.

But he also knew that the main reason behind his lack of progress was that his mind wasn't on work. His mind was on a certain unattainable widow.

He'd used patience in pursuing her, too. And had ended up losing out to a more impetuous lover. Dear God, he hoped West was careful with Caroline, or he'd beat the poltroon to a pulp and turn him into compost.

"Bugger, bugger, bugger," he muttered as he turned and knocked a stack of terracotta saucers to the tiled floor. He surveyed the shattered mess and told himself he couldn't go on like this. Other men failed in love and survived. Surely he could learn from their example.

He'd spent the last month struggling to forget Caroline Beaumont. Precious little good it had done him.

New faces, old friends, stimulating discussions, lectures, travel, research. Nothing had dislodged her from heart or mind.

He wasn't sleeping. He wasn't eating. Much more and he'd go mad indeed.

The worst of it was that none of his suffering brought him one inch closer to luring his beloved away from West. As a scientist, he admired efficiency above all. And his anguish over Caroline was the height of wastefulness. But no matter how he tried, he couldn't conquer it.

The best cure, he supposed, was to take a mistress. Or at least slake this turbulent, overpowering misery with a woman for a night. He'd reached the point of inquiring after the address of Edinburgh's most fashionable courtesan. But when the time came, he'd turned away from that discreet door to walk the dark alleys of the Old Town until dawn. He felt sick enough with himself already. Another bout of meaningless copulation in a life of meaningless copulation wouldn't cool his fever.

No, it was Caroline or nobody. God help him.

He sighed heavily and went in search of a dustpan and brush. He usually had an assistant working with him. But a few days ago he'd sent Mr. Jones on holiday, appalled to see how enthusiastically the earnest young man had grabbed the chance to escape his temperamental employer.

Yesterday Helena had tried to talk to him about his

mercurial behavior. He'd snapped her head off, too. And Dobbs had taken to lurking in the dressing room to avoid his irascible master.

At this rate, not only would Silas have no Caroline to love him, he'd have nobody at all. Right now when even breathing seemed hardly worth the effort, that didn't sound such a bad outcome.

He was on his knees sweeping up the jagged shards of orange pottery when he heard a soft footfall. Helena must have decided to venture into his cave to offer more advice. His sister wasn't noted for her prudence. He wished to hell she minded her own business.

"Helena, for God's sake…" he growled, but when he looked up, it wasn't his sister hovering near a bench packed with beakers and buckets and the detritus of the botanical-minded gentleman. "Caroline."

If he'd ever been optimistic enough to imagine that their time apart weakened his longing, one glimpse of her and he knew better. Even understanding she wasn't for him, even understanding she'd given herself to another man, his breath caught with pleasure. The morning sun through the roof lit her like an angel in stained glass. Except she was no angel. She was beguilingly, intriguingly human.

At their last meeting, they'd quarreled. He'd known at the time that his apology had been inadequate. He'd acted like a boor. These days he always acted like a boor in her presence. When all he wanted was to cherish her and place his heart at her feet and beg her to love him.

A tongue-tied boor. Damned if he could come up with another word to follow that reverent murmur of her name.

He took too long to realize that she appeared equally dumbstruck. Awkwardly he stood, shoving the dustpan onto the untidy bench. He wasn't dressed for social calls. People usually left him alone to get on with his experiments. That counted double recently when his temper was so unpredictable. His shirt was old and stained, and the nature of his work meant dirt. He wiped his hands on his sides, but he was humiliatingly conscious of black fingernails and grime on his skin. He bet bloody West could come through a tornado without picking up a speck of dust.

"Good morning, Silas," she eventually said, twining her hands in her dark green skirts. She glanced down. "You've…you've had an accident."

"I'm bungling everything lately."

Once she'd make some teasing response to that. Now she licked her lips nervously and avoided his eyes. He bit back a groan. That flicker of a pink tongue made his blood simmer. "What are you doing here, Caro?"

She raised a hand to fiddle with her rich brown hair, tortured into some elaborate style with plaits and green ribbons. His fingers—his dirty fingers—itched to pull that soft mass down around her shoulders. "I called to see Helena, and she told me you were back."

"Yes, but what are you doing *here*?"

"I wanted to talk to you." The blue eyes she raised were dull with unhappiness. She returned to twisting her skirts.

He squashed his automatic yen to comfort her. To hell with her. What right had she to be unhappy when she lay in Vernon bloody Grange's arms?

Standing so close without touching her became too tempting. Silas bent again to brushing up broken pottery. He hoped she didn't notice his unsteady hands. But if he kept looking at her, he'd grab her and kiss her and God knew what else. Any chance of keeping a civilized gloss on their dealings would vanish.

The silence hung heavy with things unspoken. He wondered if he should sign up for the Horticultural Society's camellia collecting expedition to China. With any luck, some despotic mandarin would take a dislike to his waistcoat and chop off his head. He couldn't bear to stay in England and see Caro happy with another man.

Except now he disposed of the shards and wiped his hands on a towel and took the time to study Caro, he realized that her turmoil went deeper than this passing moment. In fact, she didn't look in much better state than he did.

This wasn't the glowing creature who had knocked society for six earlier in the season. Knowing he shouldn't, but unable to stop himself, he caught one of those restless hands. "Stop tearing at your frock. You'll make a hole in it."

Her hand jerked, but she didn't pull away. She spoke in a rush. "I'm sorry for the things I said after the Oldhams' ball. I was horrible to you." She misunderstood his frown and plunged on. "Perhaps you don't remember. It's more than a month ago, after all."

Hearing she'd given herself to West? He'd carry that scar until his dying day. "I remember," he said in a low voice.

"You were kind when I was ill."

"Don't be a goose, Caro. As if I'd leave you in the lurch."

She glanced at him quickly, too quickly for him to interpret her expression. "I know. And instead of being properly grateful, I said some stupid, mean, untrue things."

Suddenly he was extremely interested. "What sort of things?"

Her hand tightened on his. How lowering for this notorious rake that the touch of her hand was more powerful than the most daring caress from any other woman.

"I lied to you."

Her voice was so muffled, he leaned in to hear. Her scent drifted toward him. Familiar. Exotic. Alluring. Lemon soap. Warmth. A hint of sexual musk that had every hair on his body standing up. "Did you?"

"Yes. West and I aren't lovers. He hasn't even kissed me."

Anger had Silas flinging away until he couldn't see her. The bitter memory of his despair this last month strangled any relief he might have felt. Anyway, what was there to be relieved about? Her plan to take West to her bed hadn't changed. This confession gave Silas a short reprieve, nothing more.

"Why in Hades are you telling me this?" he grated out, curling his hands hard over the edge of the bench. Otherwise he was likely to grab those slender shoulders and give her a good shake until she started thinking straight.

"You were so angry with me. I knew you didn't approve." Her voice developed an edge. "Although what I do with West is none of your business."

"The devil it's not."

"I shouldn't have come," she muttered. "I'd hoped we could be friends again. I hate the way that lately everything we say feels like a bullet fired from a gun."

"I'll wager talking to West is easier." He cursed the words the minute they emerged, and he turned to apologize—again. But her devastated expression choked him to silence.

"Why do you say such things? If I didn't know better, I'd think you were jealous."

"And of course, you always know better," he snapped.

She squared her shoulders and regarded him like

something slimy eating his seedlings. "I don't know what's got into you lately, Silas. I came here with nothing but good will, and now I want to clout you with a flowerpot."

He sucked in a breath, but it wasn't enough to stop him saying the last thing he wanted. "Perhaps it's too late for us to find common ground."

When her eyes darkened with renewed hurt, guilt stabbed him. "I'm truly sorry if you feel like that. Perhaps I should go." She veered toward the door with a clumsiness he'd never seen in her before, not even when she'd been near collapse at the Oldhams' ball. "I'm sorry I bothered you, Lord Stone."

Bothered him? She drove him absolutely insane. "I suppose you're going to continue with this absurd pursuit of West. You know, if he wanted you, he'd do the running."

"Perhaps he's a kinder man than you, and he's giving me time to make up my mind," she said in a thick voice.

"Like hell he is." He lunged after her and seized her arm in an implacable grip, all his honorable intentions about letting her choose her own way dissolving to ash. "In the meantime, while West dawdles, you're going without kisses. That just isn't good enough. A woman like you needs kisses. Lots of them."

She trembled in his hold. "Silas, let me go."

His grip firmed. "No true friend would want to see you deprived."

"What—"

He caught a fleeting glimpse of eyes shooting sapphire fire before the barely leashed beast inside him overpowered the last shreds of restraint. On a surge of furious triumph, he swept Caro up against his body, and his lips crashed down onto hers.

CHAPTER FIVE

*H*eat like she'd never known before engulfed Caroline. Forbidden excitement streaked through her. Good sense went up in flames as her temper and desire rose to meet Silas with equal fervor. She was lost to the storm raging between them. Anything beyond this moment faded to insignificance.

With sizzling intent, his mouth moved on hers, demanding participation. Helpless to resist, she parted her lips, sighing surrender. He dragged her closer and his tongue dipped into her mouth, making her shake with reaction. She moaned and curled her arms around his neck.

With a suddenness that left her bewildered, he jerked free. Ruthlessly he hauled her arms down. Then his hands circled her upper arms, hard enough to hold her, soft enough to feel like a caress. He glared down at her as if he hated her.

"Slap me. I deserve it," he said roughly.

She fought to find her balance. The abrupt end to that fiery kiss left her reeling.

"Curse you, I should," she hissed as her lips tingled for more kisses. She felt so torn—until this moment, she'd had no idea he even wanted to kiss her.

Well, now she knew, and the knowing was dangerous. If she had any sense, she'd scurry out of this greenhouse as fast as she could run. But confused and unsure, she lingered. Her pride had crumbled so low that right now, she almost didn't care if he kissed her in anger or pity or passion. She'd take anything as long as he didn't leave her teetering and dizzy on the edge of this chasm.

"Then do it." He still looked half mad.

She had no idea what he wanted. To send her away? To throw her onto one of those cluttered benches and toss her skirts up? The wanton image of Silas thrusting inside her made her belly twist with such anticipation, it felt like pain. A whimper escaped her as she fought the need to pull him down and kiss him until he satisfied her ravenous hunger.

"Caro, for God's sake..." His eyes were black and lightless. Deep lines extended from the corners of his lips to his nose. A muscle jerked erratically in one cheek. He looked close to shattering. After one little kiss.

She sucked in a deep breath and felt her senses expand. Silas smelled different today, his familiar male scent mixed with earth and plants. The combination was heady, made her mouth water. He smelled wild and primitive, not like the man who drank tea and traded witticisms in his sister's elegant drawing room.

She read arousal and shame in his strained features. Right now, he wanted her, and he despised himself for it. His hands tightened, and his eyes focused on her lips with such searing attention, it felt like another kiss.

"You have no right to manhandle me." She straightened and stared back at him, imperious as a queen.

"No."

The universe of despair in that one low syllable astonished her. The blood pounding in her ears made her deaf to rational thought, but in some dusty corner of her mind curiosity stirred. He wasn't acting like a man in love with another woman.

"Then release me."

Immediately she was free. She staggered and fumbled for the bench behind her. For a giddy second, she wondered if her knees would hold her up.

"Lord, Caro, forgive me," Silas said bleakly. "I'm a barbarian."

"Yes, you are." And she'd had absolutely no idea. What else was hidden under his polished exterior?

"Slap me."

"I'd love to."

He closed his eyes and stood still as a post. She stiffened her spine and drew back her hand. Her heart beat so fast, she felt lightheaded. Outrage fed frustrated desire. She couldn't precisely say why. It wasn't because he'd kissed her. Perhaps it was because this whirlwind of emotion and hunger couldn't take them anywhere, shouldn't have brought them this far. Swirling, unsatisfied cravings had her at their mercy. She hated how the force of her love left her powerless.

"Do it," he said through his teeth as she hesitated. His features tightened, but he made no attempt to defend himself.

Very well.

As Caroline swung toward him, the air swished under her hand. Only at the last instant did she slow the blow. Gently as a bird alighting on the grass, her palm landed flat on his cheek and curved to shape his face. That dear, dear face.

When she offered tenderness instead of violence, shock whipped his eyes open. She didn't know who moved first, but she was crushed against him, his arms were lashed around her, and their lips collided with blind ardor.

This kiss was unlike the first. The rage had gone. The passion burned white hot. It was completely outside Caroline's experience, for all that she'd been married ten years. This was fire and lightning, and astoundingly carnal. Open mouths joined, tongues slid and twined and danced. She'd never forget Silas's taste as long as she lived. With shaking hands, he caught her head and held her as he plumbed every inch of her mouth. She felt devoured, seized, ravished. And she adored each moment.

Eventually when the heat between them threatened to melt her into a puddle, he wrenched away. He stared down at her, his expression tormented. She shivered with fear and excitement. She'd never in her life imagined that she could drive a man mad with lust. Yet apparently she had. However unfamiliar she was with seduction, she couldn't mistake that he burned for her. All the time, her bewildered mind kept repeating, "But this is Silas."

Fury flared in his eyes, turning them brilliant gold. He gripped her shoulders. "How the hell do you *dare* to kiss me like that, then say you're going to West?"

Her eyes narrowed as the sensual mist swiftly receded under the force of his demand. Right now, she didn't want to think about West or what she wanted in the future. She didn't welcome this reminder that she'd chosen another man to be her lover. "You know, Silas, sometimes discretion is the better part of valor."

"What the deuce does that mean?" His fingers tightened, although she had no intention of retreating.

"That means every time you speak, I end up wanting to pitch you through a window. You'd be better to stop talking."

His tawny brows lowered, and the fierce glitter in his eyes made her bristle with nerves and anticipation. "I'd like to stop you talking."

She thought she now knew the power of his kiss,

but she'd had no idea. His mouth ravaged hers, and she met him each step of the way. She wasn't backing down. He wasn't going to get the better of her.

The kiss started as a battle with neither ready to declare a truce. Then in an explosive flash, it transformed into something more. A dark tide of pleasure rushed over Caroline, washing away all thoughts of winner and loser. The only thing that mattered was for Silas to keep kissing her. She clung to him, clawing at the soft linen of his shirt. She moaned with delight as he nipped at her lower lip, then returned to sweep his tongue into her mouth. Vaguely through the ferocious onslaught, she felt him shift. Then something crashed to the floor at her feet.

She closed her eyes as the sound echoed around her. What did she care if the world shattered as long as that eager mouth plundered hers? She'd never bitten anyone in her life, but she returned the favor, scraping her teeth across his jaw. His grunt of appreciation was muffled against the sleek cushion of her lips. She tugged and ripped at his shirt until finally she found the hot, smooth skin of his back. Her fingers dug deep into the pads of muscle lining his spine.

The falling sensation seemed part of the frenzy. Then her back bumped onto a hard surface. He leaned over her, flattening her against unforgiving and angular wood. She gasped, then gasped again when his hand landed hard and possessive on her breast. Sensation thundered through her like a thousand runaway horses. Her nipples, already aching, beaded to an agony of yearning.

Silas swore softly and bent forward to press between her spread legs, close to where she wanted him. But not close enough. He cradled her head, keeping it from knocking against the boards beneath her. Another whimper escaped her as a second crash resounded through the greenhouse.

A hard, insistent pulse throbbed in her lower belly. Only Silas could fill this excruciating emptiness inside her. Perhaps he knew, because he pushed forward into her mound. She shuddered in reaction and cried out, bowing up to increase the delicious pressure. She thirsted for this primitive, earthy pleasure that turned her bones to honey.

Damn this dress. Voluminous skirts hampered her access to him. If they were naked, he'd be inside her. Her stomach cramped on a thrill to think that might yet happen. When she twisted like a maddened animal to advance the contact, she tangled herself unbearably in a gown that became an instrument of torture.

She pulled away long enough to snatch a breath. She placed her palm on his chest. "Silas."

He didn't hear her as his hands feverishly stroked her breasts. She could hear his erratic panting and feel his radiating heat. He rocked slowly between her legs, torturing her with the promise of where he wanted to take her. He returned to those deep, luxuriant kisses that left her shaking.

And close to forgetting everything but her hunger for this man.

On the verge of sinking fatally into the undertow of desire, she reached up and tugged hard on his hair. He shuddered, but didn't stop. She pulled again and at last distracted him from kissing her.

"Devil take you, Caro." His voice was hoarse as if it hurt to speak. Reluctantly he lifted his head to survey her with glassy eyes.

"Silas, I can't move."

She found unworthy satisfaction in how long awareness took to penetrate his daze. "What in Hades?"

With another breath, the wildness retreated a fraction. Enough to allow her mind to register where she was and what she was doing. She glanced around and to her horror realized that he had her splayed across a workbench. During those incendiary minutes, she'd lost contact with everything solid except Silas's body against hers.

She made a dismayed sound in her throat as her appalled gaze took in the wreck surrounding them. All that crashing and banging had been Silas's botanical equipment hurtling to the floor. The greenhouse was a wilderness of spilled dirt and shredded plants and smashed glass.

"Dear Lord in heaven," she whispered in shock.

He loomed above, hands spread on the bench on either side of her. His eyes were molten caramel and the determination sparking in them suddenly made her afraid. "Take me as your lover."

"Silas—"

"Don't pretend you don't want me as much as I want you. Not after that."

She gave him a shove, but it was like trying to move the Great Pyramid with a teaspoon. "I'm not pretending anything."

When he'd touched her, she'd succumbed to madness. Now she surveyed the shambles they'd created, and grim reality cooled the fire in her blood. She made herself recall all her reasons not to give in to Silas. Principally quite how muddle-headed he made her. She could see herself reaching a point where she lived for the sound of his voice. And there was no freedom in that.

"I want you and you want me," he said urgently.

"Yes, I want you."

His eyes flared and he loomed toward her with undisguised intent. This time she punched his shoulder hard enough to elicit a grunt of discomfort. "What the deuce was that for?"

"You're not kissing me again."

"Why not?"

She punched him once more, because despite knowing that this reckless interval must end, passion's interruption left her stirred up and edgy. Her mind told her to stand up and walk out. Her sinful, hungry body wanted to lie back while he ripped away this pestilential gown and delivered the pleasure every kiss had foretold.

She hardened her jaw. "Because I'm going to be Lord West's mistress."

That uncompromising statement achieved what pummeling hadn't. He jerked upright and stepped back, regarding her like a pernicious weed invading his orchard. "What blasted rubbish is this, Caro?"

To her chagrin, it took her several clumsy moments to straighten her dress before she could sit up and meet his eyes. He looked angry again. And hurt. She curled her fists against the bare planks beneath her as she fought the need to give him anything he wanted as long as he lost that desolate expression. Definitely muddle-headed.

Even more lethal to her frail willpower, he also looked utterly magnificent. She tried to regret the destruction she'd wreaked on his clothing. She'd dragged his shirt off one shoulder, baring part of a hair-roughened chest. The shirt hung loose around his thighs where she'd torn at it to reach his skin. His silky, light brown hair fell across his forehead, leaving him deliciously ruffled. With his hands on his hips in unconscious arrogance, he looked like a swaggering pirate ready to ravish a willing captive.

Well, Caroline Beaumont was far too sensible to have any dealings with pirates. However dashing they might be. "It's not nonsense."

"Yes, it is. You want me."

"Stop saying that."

"It's true."

She sighed. Reaction set in and she suddenly felt deathly tired and disgustingly wobbly. "Of course it's true." When her mumbled admission set his eyes glittering, she raised a shaking hand to keep him away. "You're the man I want, but West is the man I need."

He frowned and that tiny muscle renewed its agitated dance in his cheek. "What the hell?"

"He's perfect for a quick affair. You're…not."

"You're deranged." He ran a hand through his hair, becoming more beguilingly disheveled.

Her mouth dried, and she swallowed to quash a pang of desire. To remind her why he wasn't for her, and to punish herself for ceding to this futile pleasure, she pointed out the facts in a flat voice. "You're in love with Fenella."

When she'd seen them dancing a month ago, she'd been so sure that was true. His unaffected shock now made her question her conclusions before he spoke. "You bloody little fool. Is that really what you think?"

His swift and scornful dismissal had her lips tightening. "You'd be perfect together."

If she kept telling herself that, she might come to accept it. That hadn't happened yet.

He watched her with an intensity that made her shiver, despite the greenhouse's humid air. "Indeed we would."

The pain of hearing her impressions confirmed

made her breath catch on an audible squeak. He continued before she could summon a response. "Which is a damned pity when I'm not in love with Fenella."

Stupid to be happy about that. Dangerous. This pendulum of emotional extremes should provide warning enough that she was better off with West. "You're not?"

"No." His smile was wry. "I'm in love with you."

Shock stopped her breathing. The words pierced her like spears. The chains squeezed clanking around her chest again, starving her lungs.

"You can't be," she said in a constricted voice.

"I can."

She'd been angry with him before. Sometimes she thought she'd been angry at him for months. Nothing matched the rage that flared at that moment. Reviving air rushed into her, lending her power to deny him. "You will not love me. I won't allow it."

He moved and she thought he meant to take her in his arms. Instead he regarded her with a masculine superiority that made her want to hit him again. "You have no power to change my feelings for you."

She brushed back the hair tumbling around her face and struggled to her feet. She hated to be cruel to him, but she had to stop him before he lured her over that deadly edge. Beneath her anger lay the old fear of being trapped the way she'd been trapped with Freddie. Her voice shook as she spoke. "You won't love me after I've given myself to West."

The line of his mouth was grim. "Yes, I will."

"And West's successor. I'm not tying myself to any one man. I did that once and I loathed it."

"Is that why you won't have me? Because you think I want forever?"

No, she wouldn't have him because she feared she was the one who might want forever. And forever was freedom's opposite. She shook her head emphatically. "I'm not going to argue about this."

"You're a coward, Caro." He didn't shift to allow her access to the door. "I never realized that before."

"That's not fair," she protested, stung. "You know what my marriage to Freddie was like."

His expression was unrelenting. "I've guessed. You've never actually told me. Every time we approach anything like a serious conversation, you change the subject."

"Then take my word for it, I'll never marry again."

"That's devilish interesting, especially as I haven't asked you."

She flinched. Another humiliation to pile on this morning's hundred other humiliations. "So when you say you love me, you mean the way you loved all those flighty widows and opera dancers?"

Bitterness edged her question. She hoped the reminder of his wicked past would make him retreat. He stayed planted in front of her, cornering her against the bench where she'd been seconds away from taking him into her body.

"I didn't love them. You're the only woman I've ever loved. And, yes, I may as well admit it, little good it will do me—you're the only woman I've ever wanted to marry."

No, no, no. She wouldn't take responsibility for his happiness. She briefly shut her eyes to close out his burning sincerity. If she could close her ears to his declarations, she'd do that, too. "I don't want you to love me," she said desperately.

"Too bad." He caught her shoulders again, more gently this time. "Caro, look me in the eye and tell me you feel nothing."

She raised her chin and met his gaze with a false show of defiance, while her heart begged her to confess her love. Ruthlessly she reminded herself how smothered she'd felt with Freddie. Living with Silas would be worse. He knew her so well that he'd see how she strained against the restrictions of marriage. And when he saw that, she'd hurt him.

Silas's eyes softened as he studied her. Briefly he was the kind, undemanding man who had brought light to the long, dark night of her mourning. "Caro?"

For one fraught instant, vows of love trembled on her lips, and she let herself imagine what it would be like to live as Silas Nash's beloved. Then very deliberately she put aside that picture and remembered her suffocating marriage, and before that life with her bully of a father. She'd dreamed of liberty for too long to relinquish it. Whatever the enticement.

"Silas, this has to end now."

"Why?"

She forced herself to give the only answer that would keep him at a distance. "I intend to arrange a rendezvous with West after his picnic at Richmond tomorrow."

Her announcement snuffed out the light in Silas's eyes and he went white. She waited for him to push her away in disgust. She hadn't answered his question, but he was so on edge, she prayed he wouldn't notice.

Instead of letting her go, his hold firmed. "Then damn you, Caroline." His voice was like gravel. "Damn you for throwing away what we could have created together."

"You have every right to be angry," she said, struggling to sound like her heart wasn't breaking. "I hope one day you'll understand." She'd reached a point where she wasn't even sure if she understood anymore.

"Then the least you can do is kiss me goodbye."

Her wayward soul, the soul convinced that rejecting Silas was a huge mistake, welcomed his embrace. She made no attempt to contain her response to his savage kiss. It was the last time before she put away her love forever and seized the life she'd always dreamed of. Those dreams had kept her going for so long. They couldn't be wrong.

"Caro…" he muttered, burying his hands in her

tangle of hair and nibbling a tantalizing line down her neck.

Sensation rippled through her, turned her blood to syrup. He edged her backward until her hips hit the bench behind her. She was nearly back to where she'd been before. She looked dazedly over his shoulder—and met Helena's interested dark gaze.

"Silas, stop," she gasped, turning rigid as a board in his hold.

"There's a reason they call them glasshouses, you know," Helena said in a mocking tone.

"Hell and damnation," Silas growled and wrenched away to face his sister. With quick protectiveness, his arm curled around Caroline.

Shame prevented Caroline from appreciating the gesture. "Let me go," she muttered, wriggling free.

Her unsteady hands rose to her bodice. Against all odds, it remained in place. Without meeting anyone's eyes, she frantically checked the chaotic greenhouse for her pelisse and reticule before remembering that she'd left them inside. She hadn't come here to see Silas—she hadn't known he'd returned from Leicestershire—but to see Helena. Helena who surveyed the two of them with arched eyebrows and an expression that combined amusement and curiosity and surprise.

"I must go." Caroline pushed past Helena and headed doggedly for the door. She cursed the shards of pottery impeding her progress, mute witness to the madness that had possessed her. She wanted to leave this greenhouse more than she wanted the hope of heaven.

Behind her, she heard Helena say to Silas, "Just what have you got to say for yourself, my dear brother?"

Caroline knew she had no right to delay outside to hear his reply, but she did. She might as well have kept going. She learned nothing new.

"Mind your own bloody business and leave me the hell alone, Helena," he snarled. Through the glass—it was mortifying quite how visible he was—Caroline watched him turn his back on his sister. He braced his arms on the workbench and dropped his head to stare at the rough boards. His stance reeked of defeat and desolation.

She'd done this to him, and she hated herself for it. On a cracked sob, Caroline turned and raced across the lawns to the house.

CHAPTER SIX

"Caro, for pity's sake, wait." Helena rushed to catch up with her as she barged through the French doors into the empty morning room.

"I have to go." The words clogged in Caroline's throat. Along with acrid tears and a lunatic yearning to run back to Silas and beg him to forgive her.

Helena caught her arm, halting her headlong flight. "You can't go out on the street like that."

"Lend me your carriage, then." How she wished she'd driven this morning, instead of walked from her house accompanied by a footman. How she wished she'd never come here at all. She struggled not to remember Silas declaring his love. Every time she did, her chest tightened to paralysis, and she felt like the real world rushed away from her down a long dark tunnel.

She battled to rein in her panic. Silas's kisses had thrilled her. His love terrified the life out of her.

"I don't think you want the servants to see you." Helena dragged her across to the mirror over the fireplace.

"Oh, dear God," Caroline whispered, appalled at what she saw. "I look like I've been romping in a hedgerow with the Household Cavalry."

Her hair flowed around her, somehow more wanton for what remained of the morning's neat coiffure. A fraying plait. A couple of pins sliding from the tangled mass. Her dress, thank heaven, was still fastened. But that was all she had to thank heaven for. The pretty green muslin was crushed and stained. Silas's teeth had left a red mark on her neck. Dirt streaked one cheek. After those fierce kisses, her lips were swollen and glistening.

"A muddy hedgerow," Helena said drily. "I'll get Rose to fix you up."

"What's the point?" Her voice was bleak. "My reputation will be in shreds anyway. If your servants saw me flat on my back, they won't keep the story to themselves. Why on earth didn't you stop us sooner?"

Helena frowned. "I thought you knew quite how public the greenhouse is."

Caroline looked away from the devastated gaze she met in the mirror and slumped onto a dark blue sofa. She could hardly believe only minutes ago, she'd been kissing Silas. Now she didn't know where to turn. "I must have been mad. All London will call me a strumpet."

Helena sat next to her and took her trembling hand. "It's not as bad as that."

"Yes, it is."

"Most of the staff have worked for us for years and they adore Silas. And hopefully they're too busy to check on what his lordship's up to in the garden."

"You're clutching at straws."

"Yes." She squeezed Caroline's hand to apologize for her bluntness. "But no point borrowing trouble. Let's get you back to your fashionable self, then we'll decide what to do."

From where she sat, Caroline had a painfully clear view of the fatal glasshouse. The kisses she and Silas had shared would have been as visible as if they stood on a stage. Bile rose in her throat at the performance they'd put on. "I can't stay. I can't face Silas."

"I suspect he'll brood in there for a while yet."

Caro's stomach soured with self-hatred as she studied that tall form. She hardly heard Helena leave the room. Instead she watched him standing hunched over the place where only minutes ago, she'd been spread out for his delectation.

Then the scoundrel had had the nerve to tell her that he loved her. She wished to heaven he hadn't. That familiar breathless feeling overwhelmed her. She made herself inhale to clear her head. And again. Already the tentacles of that precious, unwanted love reached out to throttle her dreams.

The only true liberty a well-bred woman could have was as a widow of independent fortune. After unwilling subservience to a martinet of a father, then an uncongenial, if not unkind husband, she was now in that enviable position.

So what did she do? She went and fell in love. Could she be any more of an idiot?

Today's astonishing events opened her eyes to so much. Her ability to hurt Silas. His love. The reason behind his sudden cantankerousness—however jealous she'd been of Fenella, he'd been equally jealous of West.

The invincible power of desire.

She caught her breath and closed her eyes as her body heated to the memory of those ferocious kisses. Today's encounter had held little tenderness, but dear God, they'd shared passion. A passion that threatened to set the whole world on fire.

Tears pricked her eyes. So sad that after ten years of marriage, she only just discovered desire. Now she had, could she accept its counterfeit with Lord West?

She liked West. She had little doubt that he'd prove an accomplished lover. But how she'd thrilled to Silas's shaking, desperate need. To Silas, she'd been water to a man dying of thirst. To West, she was a bonbon to sweeten a moment. Consumed, enjoyed, then forgotten.

She reminded herself that brief enjoyment was

what she required, not a love that demanded commitment and promises and duty. After those dismal years nursing Freddie, she'd decided that if she ever got the chance, she'd dance through the rest of her life like a butterfly, alighting to taste a flower's nectar, but never lingering beyond the moment.

Well, so far she was a complete failure as a creature of air and space and freedom. That went to show what a calamity love was.

She'd survived Freddie on willpower alone. Surely she could summon that will to claim the future she wanted. The first step was to move past this hankering for the man she wouldn't let herself have. At her ball, she'd felt like she had the whole world in the palm of her hand. She could feel like that again. She *would* feel like that again. But only if she took decisive action to seize her destiny.

Enough of this shillyshallying. Her new life started now.

She clenched her hands into fists and shored up her shaky resolution. With one final look at Silas, she silently said farewell to the love they might have shared if she'd been a different woman with a different past.

When Helena returned with a tea tray and Rose, her maid, Caroline already plotted the steps to Lord West's seduction.

Silas pounded on the glossy black door to the tall white house in Half Moon Street. It was too late for polite calls—but then, this wasn't a polite call. The burly night watchman halted on his rounds and raised his lantern. The cove must be shortsighted, because apparently he only saw a well-dressed representative of the upper classes, not a man with violence on his mind. He wished Silas a cheerful good evening and shuffled on his way.

Silas went back to banging on the door until Beddle, West's butler, appeared. "My lord," the man said in surprise, briefly forgetting his dignity.

Silas had known Beddle since his days as a junior footman on the Grange estate. He could forgive a little informality. "Is he in?" he barked.

Beddle looked taken aback. "It's after midnight, sir." Behind Beddle, lamps lit the elegant black and white entrance hall.

"If he's out, I'll wait." After pacing his rooms until he felt likely to lose his mind, Silas had set out on this impetuous errand to confront West. Hopefully a man who planned a day outdoors might forsake the flesh-pots and have an early night. Not to mention reserving his energy for after the picnic when he pleasured a new mistress. That thought stirred the savage beast barely restrained inside Silas.

"Please come in." Beddle's magisterial manner returned. "I'll ascertain if his lordship is at home."

"I'll wait in the library," he said, striding ahead. He

knew this house as well as he knew his own. He and West had been friends since childhood. Silas marched into the dark room and flung the curtains open. Behind him, a footman lit the lamps and set the fire.

"Brandy, my lord?" the footman asked.

Silas didn't turn from the window. "I'll see to myself, thank you."

"Very good, sir." The servant left Silas to brood.

How easily he'd fallen under the spell of his sister's lovely new friend. He wasn't a stupid man—even now, with his brain turned to sludge. He'd soon recognized that Caroline Beaumont carried wounds from her marriage. But their immediate affinity had led him to believe that with careful wooing, she'd be his.

What an arrogant coxcomb he'd been. These long months of pursuit, and all he had to show were a scarred heart, some bitter arguments, a couple of kisses more torment than pleasure, and an empty bed.

Reflected in the window he saw a man haggard with love. To escape that disagreeable image, he started to prowl around the library. A stack of correspondence waited on the imposing mahogany desk. Idly, Silas cast his eye across the letters.

What the devil? His heart crashed to a stop.

Oh, Caro. You bloody well went and did it.

He almost found himself admiring her audacity. After the confession that West hadn't kissed her, part of him had assumed that her threat this morning had been bravado.

Like hell it had been bravado.

A man's correspondence was sacrosanct. In opening that letter on top of the pile, Silas defied every rule of good manners. If anyone discovered what he'd done, he'd be drummed out of society.

Bugger good manners. Bugger society. Quickly he grabbed the note and broke the seal. A few seconds to read the contents. Another second to slip it into his pocket.

His ruin was now official. Love had brought him crashing down like all this morning's broken pots in his greenhouse. Caroline Beaumont had destroyed his principles. He deserved to be horsewhipped. Worse, he suffered not a moment's remorse over his actions.

When West arrived a few minutes later, Silas was perusing one of the crowded bookshelves on the far side of the room.

"Stone, what in Hades are you doing here at this hour?" West strode into the room and shut the door after him. "Have you had a drink?"

"No." Silas turned to glower at his host.

"Good Lord, man, you look like your dog just died. What is it?" West spoke lightly as he crossed the room to pour two brandies. Over shirt and loose trousers, he wore an extravagant green silk dressing gown patterned with entwined Chinese dragons.

Silas drew himself up to his full, impressive height, although this wasn't how he'd pictured the scene. For a start, West hadn't been dressed so casually. Nor had his manner conveyed such ease.

"I'll do everything in my power to stop you having her," he said stiffly.

West paused in passing Silas a glass and frowned. "Having who? Helena?"

"Helena?" Silas scowled at his oldest friend. "What the deuce does my sister have to do with this damned mess?"

"You'll have to make yourself clearer, old chum."

Dear God above, was the man so consumed by debauchery that he'd lost track of his paramours? Any guilt that Silas might have felt evaporated. Even if she could never be his, Caroline deserved better than this careless Lothario.

"I'm talking about Caro," he bit out, each word barbed like an arrow.

"Caro?" West looked bewildered. "You mean Caroline Beaumont?"

Silas's right hand clenched at his side. He'd dearly love to punch West's smug face. How dare this bastard bandy words with him? "Of course I bloody well mean Caroline Beaumont. Who else do you intend to take as your mistress?"

"Nobody," West said calmly, replacing the filled glass on the sideboard.

"Well, you shan't have her."

He continued to regard Silas as though a raving

lunatic ranged about his library. "Very well, I shan't have her."

Silas rose on the balls of his feet, ready to thump West. Then he realized what the man had said. He felt like someone had ripped the floor away beneath his feet. He'd come ready for an epic battle, while West seemed unconcerned to the point of ignorance.

"Damn you, is that all you have to say?"

"What do you want me to say?" With a nonchalance that rekindled Silas's itch to spill blood, he collected his brandy and wandered across to a leather chair near the fire.

"I want you to say…" Silas broke off. Actually West had said exactly what Silas had burst into this house to hear. He sucked in a deep breath and a glimmer of logic pierced his turbulent thoughts. "What in blazes is going on?"

West settled in the chair and regarded Silas with an amiable expression. "You tell me. There I was, reading the latest scandalous novel, preparing to retire to my couch in virtuous solitude, and my butler tells me Lord Stone is downstairs demanding my presence. I ask you again—why are you here?"

Silas narrowed his eyes. "You know."

West shook his dark head. "Not an inkling, my dear man. And if all you intend to do is play riddles, I must send you on your way. I'm hosting that outing to Richmond tomorrow and I want my wits about me."

Silas straightened and stared West down. "Act innocent as much as you like. I intend to fight you for Caro."

West frowned again and took a leisurely sip of his brandy. That insouciant air had annoyed Silas for months. Right now, it made him want to crown his lordship with the gilt celestial globe set on the table at his elbow.

"I'm always ready to play fisticuffs with you, Stone, even if we haven't sparred since our teens. From memory, the honors then were fairly equal."

West was one of the few men who could best Silas in a physical contest—at least until Silas had decided brawling ill befitted a man of science. "Then stand up, you bastard," Silas said belligerently.

West didn't budge. "By all means, old man. But please put me out of this agony of suspense—why have you chosen me as your punching bag, out of all the men in London?"

Silas paused in the act of raising his fists. "Caro has decided to take you as her lover."

At last, genuine emotion flashed in West's eyes. "Good Lord above, really? I had no idea."

His friend—former friend—sounded sincerely surprised. And much as Silas wanted to think West an unregenerate liar, thirty years of acquaintance told him the man was caught unawares. "You've flirted with her all season."

West shrugged and drank some more brandy. "She's a lovely creature. And entertaining besides. Of course

I've flirted with her. I never sensed any genuine interest."

Silas scowled. "She wants you in her bed."

West looked more cheerful. "Well, that's remarkably interesting."

"If you lay a finger on her, I'll tear you limb from limb."

"You'll need an army. I've kept up with my sporting pursuits. You, my boy, have wasted your youth and vigor digging neat little holes in teeny weeny flowerpots."

"I could beat you with one hand tied behind my back," Silas scoffed, while his dull, obsessed masculine brain battled to come to terms with the astounding fact that West was no rival at all.

"Only if someone cuts off my arms and legs." West rose and returned to the sideboard. He refilled his brandy, then lifted the other glass and extended it toward Silas. "Take down your fighting colors, Stone. Your lady is a prize, but she's not for me."

Without accepting the brandy, Silas surveyed West as the truth finally bashed him over the head. He'd been a blasted fool. What the hell was wrong with him? If Caro and West had shared any true attraction, they would have acted on it before this. Still, after all this time, he couldn't quite relinquish his suspicions. "You and Caro have been dancing around each other for months."

"Dancing with, not around. She's society's new

darling. Naturally I made a show of chasing her. You know the game."

He did indeed. If he hadn't been crazed by unrequited love, he'd have noted that West was too circumspect with Caro to be on the hunt.

With a growling exhalation, he let go of months of anger. "Oh, confound you, West," he said, aggression seeping away. He took the glass of brandy. "It's antics like this that get you into strife. If you could just say one word and mean it, there would be a deal less trouble in the world."

"And where would be the fun in that?"

Silas swallowed a mouthful of liquor, aware that he'd acted like an ass and grateful that West wasn't making an issue of it. The idea that he could appreciate anything West did was shocking enough to kick his brain back into action, after months of blundering around on blind instinct.

"Sit down and stop looming." West gestured to the matching leather chair as he ambled back to where he'd been sitting.

"I suppose I ought to apologize for bursting in on you." Silas took the chair and drained his glass.

West shrugged. "We all do silly things when we're in love."

Silas didn't bother arguing. It would only confirm West's opinion about the state of his emotions. "How would you know?"

A faint smile hovered around West's lips. "You'd be

surprised, old chap." Then before Silas could question that unexpected response, he went on. "Damned fine woman, Caro Beaumont. I commend your taste."

"She's damned elusive," Silas said on a sigh, tilting his head back on the chair and studying his friend from under lowered lids. "I'm devilish glad I don't need to kill you."

West gave a grunt of laughter. "Not as glad as I am." His deep voice turned thoughtful. "You know, if I was to wager on the man who's caught the delectable Lady Beaumont's interest, I'd pick you."

Silas's lips tightened. After today's kisses, and with West out of the race, so would he. "She's running scared."

Caro had looked absolutely petrified when he'd told her he loved her. One would think he'd threatened to cut her throat instead of adore her forever. If only he could convince her that love meant a richer version of freedom, not its end.

"If I'd been married to Freddie Beaumont, I'd run scared, too. Man was a witless nonentity, and it would have taken a cannon to shift him from that muddy hollow they call the family estate. Good farming country, excellent hunting, but a suffocating backwater for a lively creature like Caro."

Curiosity roused Silas from his torpor. Now that he wasn't angry with West anymore, he realized how tired he was. It had been a difficult week. Hell, it had been a difficult three months. "You knew him well?"

"We were at Harrow together. Dull as a wet week even then. Sort of blockhead who turns middle-aged before he hits twenty. Whoever put that match together was more of a blockhead than Freddie. Can't imagine the girl went after him. Freddie was never a cove to set feminine hearts aflutter."

"Her father."

"There you have it, then," West said with satisfaction.

Puzzled, Silas studied him. "There I have what exactly?"

West's sigh was tolerant. "Girl's only known blockheads when it comes to the men in her life. It's up to you to convince her not every chap is a nincompoop."

Silas turned to stare into the fire. Actually he had a horrible feeling that over the last few months, he'd been a bigger nincompoop than even the late Freddie Beaumont. "Easier said than done."

"I have every faith in you." West stood and clapped him on the shoulder. "Even if you did force your way in here, talking absolute balderdash."

CHAPTER SEVEN

*T*he morning of Lord West's picnic, Caroline crawled out of bed after a sleepless night. She felt old and tired and empty. Whenever she'd closed her eyes, she'd relived those torrid moments in Silas's arms. Staring wakeful into the darkness, she'd revisited the agony of hearing him say he loved her.

Impossible to say which was worse.

Now she jammed her turbulent misery deep down inside her, sealed tight into a corner of her soul that she never intended to visit again. She had to be ruthless and determined, or admit that the life she longed for was forever out of reach.

The first step to erase her yen for Silas Nash was consummating her affair with West, even if she felt more like a martyr facing the stake than a woman rushing into the arms of a much-desired lover. Once West shared her bed, this ridiculous second guessing must surely stop.

From the first, she'd recognized Vernon Grange as what she wanted. The only thing that had changed since was her troublesome love for Silas. A love she intended to ignore until it wilted away from neglect.

If her cowardly self secretly hoped that West would decline her offer or claim a prior engagement, that hope shriveled with the arrival of the morning's letters. They included an unsealed sheet of cream paper with "tonight" scrawled across it in a slashing masculine hand.

Stubbornness alone had Caroline making a special effort with her appearance and setting out for Richmond in her neat little curricle. Without noticeable effect, she told herself to buck up. She'd devoted more than a year to these plans. She wouldn't shirk her purpose just because she'd gone and fallen in love like a sentimental nitwit.

Oh, dear, she still sounded like she faced a hanging. Without great optimism, she hoped West's sensual skills would defeat her misgivings. He'd need to show spectacular prowess indeed to eclipse the memory of Silas's searing kisses. Who would have thought her kind, undemanding companion could set the world ablaze with a single touch?

Who would have thought such a notorious rake could fall in love?

"Oi! Watcha!"

She blinked to clear misty eyes and realized with

horror that her horses wandered all over the road and had nearly run down a thickset tradesman. Thank goodness, she was nearly at Fenella's door. Otherwise she feared for London's pedestrians.

"Caro, isn't it a lovely morning?" Fenella came tripping down the stairs of the Curzon Street house, unrecognizable as the subdued creature who had reluctantly joined their pact last February. Caroline might be an arrant failure as a dashing widow, but she was delighted to see Fenella looking so happy. Odd when not long ago, she'd wanted to scratch out Fen's bright blue eyes. Today she was just grateful that her companion on the road wasn't Helena, who knew far too much about the confusion ripping apart Caro Beaumont's heart.

"Good morning, Fen," she said, struggling to sound equally jolly.

Her friend cast her a curious look from under the brim of her stylish bonnet with its pink silk trimming. "Perfect weather for a picnic," Fenella said after a pause, living up to her reputation for tact.

Surprised, Caroline took in her surroundings. Since she'd left Helena's yesterday, she felt like a gray cloud had followed her around. But the weather was in fact glorious. During the night, she'd been craven enough to pray for heavy rain and the picnic's postponement. Or better, its complete cancellation. And not only because of her tryst with West. She dreaded discovering that her cavortings in the greenhouse had become common knowledge.

Fenella was staring with open longing at the horses instead of paying attention to her. "What high steppers."

Caroline looked at her matched chestnuts, then at her friend. "Would you like to drive?"

Pure pleasure transformed Fenella's blond prettiness to flashing beauty. "Could I?"

"As long as you promise not to land us in the ditch." She didn't mention how close she'd come to doing someone serious injury on the way.

A bit of rearranging and Fenella sat beside her, holding the ribbons with an easy competence that pierced Caroline's self-absorbed dejection. She regarded her friend with astonishment. "Good heavens, you've been hiding your light under a bushel. You're an expert."

Fenella smiled as she set the chestnuts moving. They obeyed with a smooth swiftness Caroline had never achieved. "I used to love driving. I haven't done it in years. I wasn't sure I still had the knack."

With unconcealed admiration, Caroline observed her friend as the curricle bowled along the street toward Richmond. "You certainly do."

Flicking the reins, Fenella took a sharp corner with a skill that left Caroline breathless. Who would have guessed her shy friend possessed such a talent?

"You'll be the toast of the Four-in-Hand Club."

Caroline winced to recall her ham-fisted steering earlier. "Why on earth don't you own a carriage?"

With a deftness so ingrained, she hardly noticed what she did, Fen rounded a loaded dray and steered the horses west. "I haven't taken the ribbons since Waterloo." Her voice lowered, making Caroline lean closer to hear over the traffic. "It seemed wrong to enjoy myself after Henry was gone."

Caroline sat up and looked aghast at Fen. "Henry would have hated you to give up on life."

"I wanted to. God forgive me, I wanted to. If I hadn't had Brandon, Lord knows what I'd have done. I've got you and Helena to thank for bringing me back to myself. I owe it to Brandon—and to Henry—to be more than a gray little shadow."

"You're not a gray little shadow," Caroline said, regretting how she'd dismissed Fenella as just that when they met.

"Not anymore, by heaven." With the way clear, Fenella urged the horses to a snapping pace.

Caroline looked at the lovely woman in charge of this carriage—and in charge of her life—and saw a new confidence. She'd noticed the confidence before, of course. But then she'd attributed it to Silas's love. The bitter misery trussed inside her stirred and strained against its bonds.

She bit her lip and stared hard at the road, telling herself under no circumstances would she cry. The command failed, as it had failed all through the desolate night. Luckily the fresh wind in her face whipped away any stray tear that dared to escape her iron control.

Silas arrived ahead of Caroline at West's lavish picnic beside the Thames, but not ahead of Helena. His sister must have been watching out for him, because she marched up to where he dismounted, clearly spoiling for a row. Only the presence of the groom leading his horse away delayed her attack.

"You can't run away from me forever, brother dear," Helena said, once they were alone.

If only he could. So far, he'd done an excellent job of avoiding her. Yesterday, too heartsick to face an inquisition, he'd escaped through the back gate before she could corner him. When she'd called at his rooms in the afternoon, he'd told Dobbs to say he was out. This morning, he'd chosen to ride instead of joining her in the carriage as they'd originally arranged.

He knew she was worried about him, but right now she wasn't the focus of his interest. His fight to win a certain troublesome widow was. He needed every ounce of cunning and resourcefulness to ensure his victory, and Helena's interference was an unwelcome distraction. He felt brittle and alert like a man on the eve of battle, the way he did when his experiments verged on a breakthrough.

Caroline Beaumont didn't know it yet, but her dashing days were about to end.

"Good morning to you, Hel." He shifted his gaze from where Caroline's curricle turned off the road onto the grass. "Perhaps if you looked less set on a scolding, I might be less eager to take to my heels."

"I'm not going to give you a scolding," she said, and they both heard the unspoken "even if I should" at the end of that sentence.

"You couldn't say anything that I haven't already said to myself." Caro's presence set him bristling with awareness, like a hound scenting a fox. "I have no idea what got into me yesterday."

That was a lie. He and Helena both knew what had got into him. Volcanic passion too long suppressed.

"Well, given the risks you took, you've got the devil's own luck."

"Have I?" It didn't feel that way, not after he'd told Caro he loved her and she'd thrown his words back in his teeth.

Helena must have heard the grimness underlying his question because her martial air eased. "Well, in one respect at least. A scandal's unlikely. The servants were all downstairs having their dinner when you—"

"Lost my head?"

"From what I can gather, nobody saw a thing. Which is a better outcome than you deserved. Good God, seducing Caro in a building made of glass—it beggars the imagination."

"You said no scolding, Hel."

Her lips tightened. "Very well. I imagine you've spent the night cursing yourself anyway. You don't need me to join in."

It was true. Or it had been until he'd visited West and set today's nefarious plan in train. He kicked idly at a tree root and cast Helena a sidelong glance. "What did Caro say after you took her into the house?"

She sent him a disgusted look. "I'm not going to tell you that."

"Pity. I could do with an inside track advantage." His attention returned to the neat little carriage rolling toward the picnic site and his eyebrows rose in surprise. "Good God, Fenella is quite the whip. I had no idea."

Helena turned to take in her friend's unexpected skills as a driver, but stuck to her topic. "Caro means to have West. I'll tell you that much."

A faint smile lightened Silas's expression. "There's many a slip between cup and lip."

Helena was no fool. She immediately guessed there was some scheme afoot. "What does that mean?" she asked sharply.

His smile intensified. "It means that the race is not yet over."

She touched his arm and spoke urgently. "Silas, even if you want her…"

He met her eyes, making no attempt to conceal his

emotion. "You know that it's worse than that. I love her."

Compassion softened Helena's disapproving expression. "I also know you've got some mischief in mind, but please be careful. She's nowhere near as indomitable as she acts."

"I don't intend to hurt her."

Her smile was sad. "You mightn't intend to, but that doesn't mean you won't."

"You two are being dashed unsociable," West drawled, prowling up behind Silas. "Save the family reunion for your own time. I've got a dozen footmen standing idle, ready to answer every whim. If you persist in loitering over here in isolation, you'll hurt their feelings."

"West," Silas said, and caught his sister's surprise at the greeting's lack of hostility. "You've been deuced fortunate with the sunshine."

"I have contacts in high places."

"More likely down below," Helena muttered. His sister was the only person Silas knew who didn't melt under West's famous charm. West had introduced Helena to his great chum, Lord Crewe, and she'd never forgiven him.

West bowed over Helena's hand and sent her a glinting glance from beneath his heavy eyelids. "Put away your barbs, my prickly lady. It's too nice a day for sniping."

Something in West's voice pierced Silas's preoccupation with Caro. Some hint of…not quite fondness. Perhaps masculine interest. Helena was an attractive woman, and West flirted with anything in skirts. But now Silas looked closely, the predatory spark in West's eyes made him distinctly uneasy.

He frowned at his friend, suddenly recalling a slip that at the time, he'd disregarded in his extremity. When he'd blundered into West's house breathing fire and vowing destruction, the first woman his friend had mentioned hadn't been Caroline Beaumont, but Helena.

Had rakish Vernon Grange set his sights on Helena Wade? And if he had, how did Silas feel about it? More importantly, how would Helena feel about it?

Silas looked at his sister and had to admit he had no idea.

Coolly she withdrew her hand. "I'd imagined more guests, my lord."

The gathering at this *fête champêtre* was smaller than Silas had expected, too, almost…intimate. West, Helena, Silas, a couple of West's raffish friends, and the freshly arrived Caroline and Fenella. Did today mark the beginning of West's pursuit? Devil take the man, if he hurt Helena, Silas *would* turn him into compost.

West shrugged. "The numbers are sufficient to my entertainment." He regarded Helena searchingly. "And hopefully yours. You didn't ride?"

"No." She directed a flash of annoyance at Silas. He

knew she'd planned to use the carriage trip to Richmond to quiz him about Caroline.

"I have a spare horse," West said.

Across the lush green field, Caro stepped out of her curricle and headed in their direction. Then she noticed Silas standing beside Helena and veered away. After yesterday's indiscretions, she must have decided evasion was the best policy.

"The perfect host," Silas said sardonically as he put aside questions about West's romantic ambitions. He had his hands full catching Caro. Unraveling his sister's intrigues would have to wait.

"I can't ride astride," Helena said. "Even in Richmond that would cause talk. But thank you for offering."

West smiled at her, and the unabashed affection in his face heightened Silas's suspicions. "When you were an impudent schoolgirl in plaits and a muddy pinafore, you used to ride astride."

She didn't smile back. "I used to do many things. But wisdom has a grim habit of following on from reckless decisions."

West's amusement faded. "Not always."

"No, not always." Fleetingly the late Lord Crewe's ghost hovered over the three of them. Like West, he'd been a man of charm and daring—and cruel selfishness that had left Helena forever scarred.

Silas watched West shake off the dark memories and become once again the urbane gentleman who had graced a thousand elegant drawing rooms. "What a shame that you won't ride when I planned this picnic purely for the pleasure of seeing you flying across the grass on the back of a fine horse."

Helena looked astonished. Likely she'd imagined he'd put this party together for Caro's sake. "Really?"

"Yes, really. It's been a fancy of mine since I saw you restricted to a trot in Hyde Park. The experience was most uncongenial for an observer. You looked like someone was strangling you. Slowly."

West was right. She only ever came truly alive galloping hell for leather over an open field. "I've missed seeing you on a horse, Hel," Silas said.

Helena frowned. She wouldn't like West's attention centering on her. Especially when his conclusions were so accurate. She preferred to play her cards close to her chest. "Town isn't the place to ride neck or nothing. I'll soon be back at Cranham."

West raised a hand toward the grooms holding the horses. "Such a pity."

"That I'm leaving London?"

"No, that you don't want a good gallop when I went to such trouble to bring you a suitable mount—and a suitable saddle."

A groom led a spectacular white mare toward them. Silas noted the Arab's proud carriage, the gleaming sidesaddle, and also the way Helena's hand curled at her side as if it already held a crop. Whatever her doubts about the man offering the favor, Silas could see that she itched to throw herself onto the lovely horse.

"What a beauty," Silas said. Like Helena, he'd been set on his first pony when he was toddling.

The groom passed the reins to West, bowed and left. The horse's ears flickered and her great dark eyes shone. She bent her noble head to nudge Helena as if inviting her to climb into the saddle.

West's thin, expressive mouth stretched into a sardonic smile. "If you deny me now, Helena, I'll think that you don't like me."

"I don't," she said shortly, cupping one hand under the horse's jaw and giving her a scratch.

"Ouch."

Deciding that West and Helena could settle into bickering without his assistance, Silas wandered toward Caroline. Without seeming to pay him any heed, Caroline turned the opposite way. He cast her a knowing glance, but lingered to compliment Fenella on her driving.

Caro glanced back before inserting herself into a group of West's friends. One step to the right. One step to the left. The day promised to play out like a children's game of dodge and catch. With, if Silas had his way, a breathtakingly adult conclusion after the sun went down.

～

Caroline's turmoil left her incapable of appreciating the al fresco party's elaborate arrangements. The string quartet under the spreading oak might as well be nails scratching on tin. The tables festooned with garlands and damask linens made no impression. The delicacies the liveried footmen served were bark and ash, for all she tasted of them.

Last night, she'd written to West in the frantic hope that she'd feel bold and independent—and free of Silas Nash. But she didn't feel brave and powerful. Instead she was a vulnerable woman rushing headlong into a future she no longer wanted. She'd been so set on becoming a dashing widow, and it turned out that she was a pitiful coward. Silas was right about her.

Nonetheless, West's circumspect behavior left her bewildered. Caroline hadn't expected overt advances, but as the day progressed, the absence of any signs of anticipation started to grate. No wink. No special smile. Not even the occasional double entendre. He treated her as he always had, like an attractive woman who aroused admiration, but no urge to overstep the bounds of propriety. If his note wasn't folded in her reticule, she'd wonder if they'd made a rendezvous at all.

Silas's behavior, too, left her floundering. After she'd told him she meant to have West, they'd parted in bitterness. She'd imagine after that, he'd be eager to avoid her. But all day she flitted from guest to guest a pace ahead of him. Whenever she saw him across the field or, worse, sauntering in her direction, her stomach clenched with humiliation and anger and forbidden longing.

The happy laughter around her indicated that everyone else was having a marvelous time. West had gone to great lengths to provide his guests with a memorable day. There were two skiffs for sailing on the river, and open carriages for excursions along the banks. He'd set up a flowery bower with cushions and rugs fit for a sultan. Inside, Helena and Fenella escaped the sun to recline on divans, while West's friends lolled at their feet like adoring slaves. West himself slouched against the pole holding up the entrance, studying Helena as if she was the most fascinating creature he'd ever seen.

Caroline stopped near her curricle to glower at him. Surely he took discretion too far. For heaven's sake, she was the lady he bedded tonight, not Helena Wade. He'd already spent a good hour galloping over the fields in her friend's company, and he'd hardly parted from her side since.

"Smile, darling," a velvety baritone murmured behind her. "The world mightn't end tomorrow."

She started and battled to control the tide of heat engulfing her. How galling that Silas had managed to sneak up on her. She'd spent all day preternaturally aware of him and doing her best to keep her distance. But for once, the reliable prickle between her shoulder blades had let her down.

Silas stood beside her and passed across a glass of champagne. Despite the extravagant selection of wines, she'd refrained from drinking. If she turned to alcohol to drown her confusion and misery, she feared she wouldn't stop. And she refused to greet her first lover in an inebriated haze.

Her bugbear lifted his glass to his lips and propped one shoulder against the side of the carriage from which she'd just retrieved a scarf. The advancing afternoon grew cool—or at least it had until she'd needed to pretend insouciance with a man who, twenty-four hours ago, had been fondling her breasts.

"Lord Stone," she said flatly, knowing her formality was absurd.

He clearly thought so, too, because his remarkable eyes lit with laughter. "My dear Lady Beaumont, what a glorious boon for your humble petitioner to surprise you adorning this verdant setting like a coy nymph awaiting the attentions of great Apollo."

Caroline scowled at him, unamused by his florid imitation of a character in a bad play. "You think you're so funny, don't you?"

The laughter seeped from his eyes, replaced by concern. "I wanted to ask if you were all right after…yesterday."

"Perfectly," she said tightly, although he'd recognize the lie.

"Did Helena tell you that your reputation is safe? The servants were downstairs when we—"

Call her reckless, but right now, looming scandal was the least of her worries. She spoke quickly before Silas put her lapse into words. "I don't have to ask how you are. You're obviously in the pink of health."

Yesterday when she'd announced that her plans for West hadn't changed, he'd looked like every hope crumbled to dust. Today he seemed his usual easygoing self. She didn't want him unhappy—she wasn't that much of a witch—but his cheerfulness was puzzling and a tad insulting. Surely a man hopelessly in love should pine just a little.

"No use crying for the moon," he said with one of those characteristic shrugs that she'd once found charming.

Well, wasn't he the absolute limit? "You're accepting your rejection in good spirit."

He took another sip of wine. "No point going into a decline."

"Indeed."

"If it would help for me to make sheep's eyes at you and droop over the scenery like some milksop in a poem, I'm at your service." She wasn't sure how he achieved it, but his tall, vigorous form stooped and his expression fell into lines of theatrical misery. "Oh, cruel mistress, your eternal coldness rends my tender heart."

"Stop it."

"I will if you kiss me better." He widened his eyes and batted his thick tawny lashes.

Despite her wretchedness, Caroline couldn't help laughing at the woebegone picture he presented. "You're a lunatic."

"Does that mean you take pity on your languishing admirer?" He clapped his hand to his chest, forgetting the champagne he held. Wine sloshed over his teal silk waistcoat. "Blast."

This time her laugh was more robust and when his eyes met hers, he burst out laughing, too. "I hope you don't expect me to moon around after you, sighing and kissing the hem of your skirt. I'd never make such an infernal cake of myself."

She set her glass of champagne on the carriage's step and dug in her reticule for a handkerchief. She was dabbing at the damp stain before she realized what she did. She was almost...wifely. How utterly revolting. On a dismayed gasp, she jerked her hand away. "I'm sorry."

His eyes softened as he caught her wrist. "No need to apologize."

"Yes, there is," she said disconsolately, scrunching the sodden handkerchief into a ball. He must feel her pulse race beneath his fingers. But then, after yesterday, the biggest dunderhead in England would know she wanted him. And nobody had ever called Silas Nash that. "I'm acting as if we're intimate. It's not fair."

"Caro—"

She wrenched away and buried her shaking hands in her yellow skirts. "I think...I think it would be better if you and I keep our contact to a minimum in future."

"My dear—"

"No, don't dear or darling or Caro me. It only prolongs the torture." She blinked back the tears that had hovered all day, even when she'd laughed at his antics. "Just let me go."

His face was stern as she'd never seen it. With a pang, she admitted that she'd misjudged him. Beneath his apparent geniality, he was wretched. Of course he was. She didn't discount the power of his love. It would be so much easier if she did. And the circumstances were all so impossible. A brief affair with Silas would be damaging enough. But her instincts screamed that he offered more, something important and profound and lasting—and that more would lock her back into the prison she'd escaped with Freddie's death.

"It doesn't have to be like this," he said gently.

"Yes, it does." Blindly she turned and stumbled away before she sacrificed everything she'd always wanted and admitted that she loved him, too.

The bedrooms in the Red Lion, the best hostelry in Kingston Upon Thames, were cavernous. When Caroline hesitantly ventured through the door connecting her chamber with the one she'd asked Hunter to reserve for West, a blazing fire and a branch of candles on a carved chest provided inadequate light.

The dusky intimacy surprised her, although she

supposed it promoted seduction. Again she regretted how unpracticed she was when it came to intrigue. She'd expected to find a bright room and a fully clothed West waiting with wine and a meal. The idea that he intended to tumble her into bed with no preliminaries shrank her faltering courage to almost nothing.

The room was quiet. Fleetingly, she wondered if West was even present, until her eyes fell on the clothing slung across a carved oak chair and the damp towel hanging from the washstand. The bed was massive to fit its surroundings, and while its curtains weren't fully drawn, the shadows behind them were thick enough to hide an elephant.

In a way, she was grateful she couldn't see Lord West. This would be hard enough without having to look into his eyes. She straightened like a soldier on parade and stared unblinking into the gloom.

"My lord, I'm so sorry. I've brought you here expecting..." She stilled the shaking hands twining at her waist. She might be a henwit, but she refused to play the nervous ninny as well. She steadied her voice. "West, I've changed my mind. I can't blame you if you're angry. I've led you on appallingly. I've disappointed myself, too. But I can't...I can't join you in that bed tonight."

She waited for some response, but the room remained ominously silent. She licked her lips and plowed on, but now nothing kept the quaver from her voice. "I hope you'll find it in your heart to forgive me. I can't explain, except to tell you that I spent my year of mourning imagining a lover just like you. That fantasy has carried me further along the path to surrender than I find I can countenance. I so wanted to be the sort of woman who embarks on a wild, passionate affair with a rake. But wanting to be someone and actually being someone are two radically different things, I've discovered. And despite all my bold talk, I'm not that woman."

No answer yet. He must be fuming. She couldn't blame him. She braced to make the final confession. The words she hated to say, even in her own mind. "I'm in love with someone else, you see. I don't want that either, but I can't seem to change it."

Did the man in the bed move? It was too dark to be sure.

When he still didn't respond, she pressed on doggedly. This encounter became even more awkward than she'd expected. And she'd expected agonies beyond description.

Her voice dwindled to a thread. "Because...because I'm in love with another man, it's not right to give myself to a man I don't love."

There. She'd set out the humiliating truth. Surely he'd speak now.

Her hands curled in her crumpled yellow skirts. This was the dress she'd worn to the picnic, although she'd changed her half boots for satin slippers. The sheer silk nightgown she'd purchased six months ago for her descent into sin remained folded at the bottom of her valise. She doubted she'd ever wear it now.

The silence extended, became oppressive. The shadows flickering against the acres of coffered ceiling turned menacing. The wind rattled the windows—the beautiful day had turned into a chilly night. A horrid thought rose in Caroline's mind.

Had West gone to sleep waiting for her? It wasn't particularly late, but she'd loitered like a coward before coming in. The prospect of having to repeat her excruciating little speech made her queasy.

Hesitantly, she stepped toward the bed. "My lord, did you hear me?"

The mattress creaked as the man in the bed shifted again. With a rattle, he pushed the curtains back and sat up, placing his bare feet on the floor. He set his hands flat on his powerful thighs and turned his head in her direction. Somber hazel eyes studied her from across the room.

"Who are you in love with, Caro?"

CHAPTER EIGHT

"*S*ilas?"

Shock crushed every other reaction, even outrage. Caroline felt like she'd set out on a stroll to the end of the garden and landed on the moon instead.

"Yes, it's me." His voice held a grim note, and his stern expression was familiar from the picnic.

"What are you doing here?" She remained too bewildered to make sense of his presence. "Where's Lord West?"

"Safely back in London, as far as I know." Silas rose, but was wise enough not to approach her. He was in shirtsleeves, and he'd changed from breeches to loose trousers. With a sick feeling, she realized she'd been stupid—again. The coat on the chair was dark brown. West's coat today had been blue.

Finally anger stirred and pushed through her confusion to become paramount. Anger and a crushing humiliation that felt like a physical blow. "So you've been playing with me all this time. You and West must have had a good laugh, but you'll forgive me if I don't find it particularly amusing."

He looked horrified. "There's no joke, damn it."

"There certainly isn't." Hot tears stung her eyes. Compared to the enormity of Silas's betrayal, West's was no worse than a mosquito bite. Another sign that love was the work of the devil. "Just a pair of spoiled and spiteful boys toying with a lady, the way they'd pull the wings off a fly. I thought better of you, Silas."

Anguished regret tightened his features, and he took a convulsive step toward her. "Caro, no, you mistake me."

"I certainly have in the past," she said bitterly. "Well, you've both had your fun at my expense. I'm delighted I provided such fine entertainment. Now I wish you good night."

She stumbled back toward her room. Luckily she'd left the door open when she came in. In her current state, she didn't trust herself to negotiate the simple mechanics of the latch.

"Caro, wait."

"No," she said in a constricted voice. How could he do this to her? Whatever sins she'd ascribed to him, she'd never thought he'd be wantonly cruel.

"Please."

Despite her frantic need to hide away with her

misery, something in his voice made her hesitate. He sounded much nearer. She braced for him to touch her, knowing her brittle control would disintegrate if he did. But instead, he reached past her to draw the door shut.

She stared unseeingly at the varnished wooden barrier. "You can't trap me in here."

"You're free to go."

She wasn't sure she believed him. But when she placed one hand on the door and pushed, he didn't move to stop her. Behind her, she heard him sigh, the sound weighted with a regret that made her wonder if she'd mistaken his motives. Then she pictured him conspiring with West to dole out her favors between them and her hand fisted against the wood.

"Please let me explain," he said softly.

"You just want to mock me," she said thickly. She was trembling as if she had a fever. Strangely while escape lay inches away behind a stout door with a key to keep him out, she didn't move. She lowered her hand to bury it in her skirts.

"On my honor, no."

On a burst of hurt fury, she whirled to face him. "You owe me better than this."

He raked a shaking hand through his thick tawny hair, and even angry as she was, she recognized his remorse. His face was pale and drawn and a muscle flickered in his lean cheek. "I do."

The soft admission of wrongdoing made her

stomach clench. "I never want to see you or Lord West again. You are both beneath contempt."

Silas's shoulders slumped and he turned away to collapse into a chair. "I've made such a hellish mess of all this." His eyes, dull with regret, focused on her. "Don't blame West. This is all my doing."

"He told you of our rendezvous."

"No, he didn't."

She frowned, backing against the door, although he didn't budge from the chair. "Then how did you know I'd be here? You didn't follow me from Richmond. You arrived at the inn before I did."

The guilt in Silas's expression intensified. "I stole your note before West read it."

She'd taken a step toward him before she remembered that he was the enemy. "But how?"

Silas ran his hand through his hair again and his gaze settled on her with a bleak resignation that, despite everything, made her want to take him into her arms. "You'll loathe me."

"Probably," she said, while her rage evaporated drop by drop. With each second, it grew more difficult to believe that his wretchedness stemmed from a nasty prank gone awry. She missed her anger. It lent her a strength she feared she was going to need. "Silas, tell me."

He firmed his jaw. That little muscle in his cheek still danced. Whatever this was, it wasn't a joke. He looked as austere as a funeral. "I went to West's house last night to challenge him for you."

"You went—" Caroline needn't have worried about her absent anger. Her breath escaped with an indignant huff. "The devil you did. I don't belong to either of you, and I don't appreciate being the subject of asinine male contests."

Gloomily he examined the rush matting covering the floor. "I knew you'd hate it."

She shifted closer. Mere feet now separated them. "What on earth did you think to achieve?"

One elegant hand made a dejected gesture. "I know it's mad. I know if you really wanted West, I could beat him to porridge and it wouldn't make a jot of difference to the outcome." He settled a blistering gaze upon her. "But you've driven me insane ever since I met you, Caro. Have an ounce of pity for a poor fellow out of his head with unrequited love."

She really didn't want to soften. She really, really didn't. All his palpable misery and declarations of love didn't alter his unsuitability as a temporary lover. Yet her traitorous heart swelled at his grudging admission. When she'd met Silas, he'd been such a model of common sense and gentlemanly behavior. She dared any woman alive to resist feeling flattered to know she'd turned that self-sufficient rake into this wreck.

"Something's definitely unhinged you."

His relentless gaze drilled through her. "Love. It's a confounded disaster."

She couldn't argue. She'd suffered a few unhinged

moments herself. She folded her arms in front of her to try and hide how she was shaking. "Go on. You may as well tell me the rest."

Silas's lips turned down. "West laughed at me, told me I was an idiot."

"He was right."

Silas ignored her remark. "He might have been less amused if he knew I'd broken his trust and read his mail. Worse, stolen it so he never knew you'd written to him."

"That was low," she said, trying to summon appropriate disgust. Silas's love must be mighty indeed if it drove him to such lengths.

He buried his face in his hands. His voice emerged as a gruff undertone. "The worst of it is I'd do it again."

"If I mean to have West, I'll have him." She struggled to sound like that might still happen, when she knew the moment for taking Vernon Grange into her bed had passed, if it had ever existed at all.

Slowly he raised his head and for the first time, his eyes held a speculative glint instead of an ocean of self-castigation. In an instant, the balance of power in the room shifted, like an earthquake beneath her feet. Her fingers clenched in her skirts as icy trepidation slithered down her spine. Any advantage that his confession had given her now disappeared.

His regard was penetrating. "Yet it seems you don't want him."

She swallowed, cursing that Silas had heard her

pathetic ramblings. "You make too much of what I said in the grip of temporary panic."

He definitely came back to himself. His hands curled over the arms of the chair and he sat straighter. "You didn't sound panicked."

"Never mind that." Nervously she saw that she'd ventured close enough for him to catch. She retreated a shaky step and stood shifting her weight from foot to foot. "You've behaved disgracefully. What did you imagine would happen when I discovered you in West's place? That I'd just smile and shrug and throw myself into your arms?"

"A man can hope."

"A man would be a fool if he did."

He stood and despite the distance between them, his height left her feeling intolerably dominated. Intolerably dominated, but alive with excitement. She shivered as she recalled yesterday's incendiary kisses. His intent expression indicated he too remembered.

A wry smile lightened his face. "I am a fool. Your fool."

"Stop it. You don't mean it." She faltered back another step, berating herself for failing to run when he was too sunk in despair to follow. He no longer looked ready to cut his throat for his sins against Caroline Beaumont.

Instead, he looked...predatory.

"Yes, I do." He loomed closer. "Who are you in love with, Caro?"

"West," she said, tilting her chin in defiance.

He laughed softly and shook his head. "No, that bird won't fly, my darling. You said too much in that touching little recitation."

Mortifyingly true. She narrowed her eyes on the tall man prowling toward her. "I don't see what business it is of yours. You're a mere acquaintance."

He shook his head again, those perceptive eyes fixed on her in a way that made her skin prickle with dread. And anticipation. "Fie, Lady Beaumont. Only a hardened flirt would kiss a mere acquaintance the way you kissed me yesterday."

Her cheeks heated. Of all the men in the world, Silas Nash alone put her to the blush. Argument enough, should she need another, to avoid him. "A gentleman wouldn't mention that unfortunate incident."

"It wasn't unfortunate." He bared straight white teeth in a wolfish smile.

She'd called him piratical yesterday. She'd had no idea. Her silly heart was beating so fast, she felt dizzy. "Good God, Silas, you were close to having me in your greenhouse, with every kiss on show to the world and his wife. The whole thing couldn't be much more unfortunate."

"And of course you're in love with another man."

"Of...of course," she said, cursing the betraying stammer.

"Yet still you mean to give yourself to West. What's the matter with your beloved?"

Right now she could compile a long list of what was the matter with her beloved. Starting with his arrogance and his determination to plumb all her secrets. "He's…he's unavailable."

Silas's eyes held a wicked light, and the flashing smile didn't fade. "So you require a stopgap?"

Seriously apprehensive now, Caroline retreated further. "That's hardly flattering—to Lord West or to me."

He followed her. "Yet true."

"Perhaps. As I said to you when I launched this bedamned enterprise, I'm looking for some adventure, not a lifelong attachment."

He stopped and spread his arms wide, the stance opening his shirt over his powerful chest. "In that case, and in West's absence, I offer myself."

He looked utterly delicious. Every drop of moisture in her mouth evaporated, and she fisted her hands to stop them from reaching toward that impressively muscled expanse of skin.

She sucked in a breath and stepped to the side. He followed. She returned to her original spot. So did he. It was like a courtly dance, a reminder of how she'd spent most of the day trying to skip out of his grasp. And hadn't that turned out a complete waste of effort? Here she was at his mercy, with nobody to blame but herself. After all, he'd given her the chance to leave and she hadn't taken it.

"You won't do, Silas," she said, hoping she sounded more convincing to him than she did in her own ears.

She waited for pique, but he continued to fix that unsettling concentration upon her. "Why not? I promise to show you pleasure. Good God, the heat between us could spark a second fire of London. Yesterday, we were mad for each other."

"Mad anyway," she muttered, bumping hard against the wall behind her.

He sighed. "Caro, I'm here. You're here. We want each other." He paused as if waiting for another denial, but what was the point? They both knew the woman in his arms yesterday had been incandescent with desire. "You want excitement. I'm happy to supply it. Let's go to bed."

Floundering for arguments to win a point she was close to forgetting, she made a helpless gesture. "This could destroy our friendship."

His expression softened and briefly he didn't look like a hungry wolf, but like her dear friend. "There is no woman I esteem as highly as you."

She struggled to remember why sleeping with Silas was a bad idea. "Then don't you think...relations between us will ruin that trust?"

"I think *relations*..." He gave the word the same shaky emphasis she had. "..between us will be richer and sweeter because of that trust."

She turned her head and gazed longingly at the door. Only a few feet away, yet it might as well be a hundred miles. "You have no respect for the women you bed."

Comprehension widened his hazel eyes. "Is that the problem?"

"One of them," she admitted in an unsteady voice. "You never take your amours seriously."

She waited for him to tell her he loved her, but to her surprise—and chagrin—laughter lit his face. "My dear Caro, you appear woefully confused. If you want a short affair, surely it's best if I don't take our liaison seriously."

She made a low sound of irritation. "You twist my words."

"Then let's stop talking altogether. You want a lover. I'm eminently qualified. Stop all this havering, sweetheart, and come to bed."

The shaming truth was that Caroline was powerfully tempted. Beyond tempted. She teetered on the brink of a decision that had once been unthinkable. But how could she resist him? It was difficult enough when she was alone to remember how wrong he was for her. When he stood before her, tall, lean, virile, willing, her longing outstripped good sense.

She waited for the familiar suffocated feeling to return, to remind her why surrendering to this one man meant death to all her dreams. To her surprise, the feeling stayed away. While her heart was racing, her breathing remained unrestricted. At this moment, the problem was that all her dreams focused on Silas Nash.

"You make it sound so simple."

"Isn't it? I want you. I hope…I believe you want me. We owe nobody else our loyalty."

She had a nasty inkling that they both knew she fought a losing battle. "I couldn't bear you to dismiss me as yet another girl Lord Stone has made silly."

The warmth in his eyes had her heart turning pirouettes. "Do I make you silly?"

"You know you do," she said with stark honesty. Heaven help her. She rapidly reached a point where retreating wasn't an option.

His smile was sweet and reminded her of his care for a lonely widow new to London. "Well, that's a relief. You've sent me silly for months."

Oh, dear, her resolution now clung only by its fingertips. "I have a question."

"Ask me anything."

"Does Mr. Harslett really seek his mother's approval for his mistresses?"

The abrupt change of topic disoriented him, then left him shamefaced. He shook his head. "No."

"I've had trouble even looking at him since you told me that."

"I'm sorry."

"And Harry Hall washes?"

"As far as I'm aware. It's not like I've questioned the fellow's valet." He shuffled his feet and she tried not to find his embarrassment charming. Tried and failed. He frowned at her. "Hell, Caroline, I said you drove me mad. There's proof of it. I've acted like a louse, maligning good men whose only fault is that you expressed an interest in them. I should be flogged."

"Perhaps that's a little extreme." She'd been flattered to learn of the stolen letter. Hearing that he'd lied about his friends to keep her from their clutches shouldn't leave her equally flattered. But it did.

Something in her tone must have encouraged him because he glanced up with a pleading light in his eyes. "My only excuse is that I love you to distraction."

Oh, he was a temptation. And despite all her flutterings and evasions, she had a strong suspicion she was about to succumb at last. "That's no excuse."

"Perhaps not. But I promise to make it up to you in that bed. After yesterday, aren't you curious about what it would be like between us?"

So curious she'd stayed awake all night, restless and hungry for more of his touch, even while she'd steeled herself to go to West. "You make it hard to say no."

"I hope so."

She tried not to smile. "If you kissed me, your victory would be assured."

She thought he'd seize her then, but she'd underestimated him. To her astonishment, he raised his hand as if to ward off an attack. "I know you too well, Caro. You'll never forgive yourself or me if you don't consent with heart and mind united."

"My body wants you. Isn't that enough?" she asked softly, shifting away from the wall until she stood in front of him.

He closed his eyes. "By God, woman, you set yourself to torment me. Is that yes?"

Troubled, she studied him. He'd won, but she conceded very much against her better judgment. All the barriers to an affair with Silas remained—except that when he stood here like this, loving her and desperate, those barriers didn't seem nearly as impassable. "It's a request for you to make the decision."

"That's like asking the mouse to take charge of the key to the cheese cupboard."

She made a frustrated sound. "God give me strength. You're *so* annoying. After behaving like a complete scoundrel, now you discover your honor. You're not proving a convenient lover, Silas."

Regretfully he stared back. "I have to agree." He studied her as if he read every fear lurking in her heart. "But I want you to be sure."

Genuine confusion flooded her. "How can I be sure?"

He reached toward her face, but stopped before making contact. "Tell me what you're afraid of."

She abandoned pride. "I'm afraid if we do this, you won't be my friend anymore."

"I'll always be on your side, whatever happens."

"Even if I take another lover?"

Something dark and primitive moved in his hazel

eyes, but his voice remained steady. "I can't lie and say I'll like that. I vow I'll make you so happy that you'll never think of leaving. But my love isn't a prison. You're free to choose what you do."

Deep within Caroline, a delicate seedling of hope unfurled toward the sun. Could she do this? Was Silas the one man in a million who could want a woman without caging her?

"What else are you afraid of?" he asked softly.

"That you'll want more of me than I'm willing to give."

He shrugged, the gesture so characteristic that her heart somersaulted with love. "I swear on everything I hold holy that I respect your sovereign soul. I'll take what you give and I won't badger you for more. Nor will I throw jealous tantrums, although after my recent behavior, you might find that hard to believe."

She regarded him doubtfully. "So no jealousy?"

His smile was crooked. "I can't promise that, but if the circumstances arise, I'll deal with it. I'm merely human. Let's make a pact. If I behave like a grumpy, possessive brute, you have the right to terminate our arrangement without a word of apology. I'll put that in writing if necessary."

"I trust your word." Despite all his devious antics to bring her to this pass, she did.

"Good. What else?"

This was the most difficult issue. "I'm afraid that I'll want more of *you* than you're willing to give me."

His smile was gentle and at last he completed the caress, cupping her jaw with a tenderness that melted her bones. "Trust me. Trust yourself. We'll come through."

Uncertainly she met his eyes, more gold than green in the candlelight. She wanted to trust him. Oh, how she wanted to. But her freedom was too dearly won to surrender easily.

"One night," she whispered, even as she leaned into his hand.

She waited for an argument, but after a pause, he nodded briefly. "One night."

"Just one," she said, surprised he accepted the limits she placed on their affair.

"*One* night," he repeated in seeming agreement. He looked as if he made an eternal vow. Before she could question the emphasis he placed on the first word, he went on. "Let me show you what joy a lover can bring you."

Accepting his offer was utterly terrifying, like crossing a gaping chasm. She spanned it with one step and went eagerly into Silas's arms.

Caroline might call herself a dashing widow, but when she linked her hands around his neck, she felt as flustered and excited as an untried girl. "Kiss me, Silas."

CHAPTER NINE

*B*ecause rushing seemed like blasphemy on this strangely sacred occasion, Silas slowly bent his head and placed his lips on Caroline's in a kiss that was almost chaste. At last she'd consented. He'd been so sure this moment would never come.

Her lushly curved body rested against his before she strained up to deepen the contact. Teasing her, he brushed his lips across hers again and again.

Eventually she leaned back to see his face. To his delight, her expression held no reticence, just curiosity and a stirring sensuality that made him hard. "I know you can do better than that."

"Aren't you enjoying it?"

"Of course I am, but perhaps it's time to get to the good stuff." Her pout did nothing for his precarious control. "We've only got one night."

Over his dead body. "Caro, stop trying to direct

events. I'm your lover, not the steward on your estate awaiting daily orders."

"But, Silas—"

He hauled her up against him and took her mouth in the kind of kiss that shook empires. She stiffened in shock before on a moan, she kissed him back. After yesterday's fierceness, he should know what to expect from her passion. But her reckless ardor sent his heart crashing against his ribs. He lost himself in a succulent heaven of satiny lips and flickering tongues and nipping teeth. When he raised his head, they were both breathless.

"Shall I take down my hair?" she asked huskily, releasing his shoulders.

"Let me." He caught her hands and placed quick kisses on each set of knuckles. "I've waited for this since I first met you."

"Really?" she asked in a wondering tone. "I had no idea."

He slid a pin from the rich brown hair. One long lock snaked across her round bosom. In a disgustingly adolescent fashion, his heart skipped a beat. "I know."

She stared at him with wide blue eyes. "You wooed me all that time."

"I did." Another pin. Another loosened lock.

"I didn't realize I was…interested in you until I thought you were in love with Fenella—then I wanted to kill you both."

His lips twitched. "How appalling."

She regarded him wryly. "You know I'm no angel."

"For which I'm heartily grateful."

Another pin free. Then another. And another. The fashionable coronet started to look alluringly disheveled.

The simple act of undoing Caroline's hair threatened to bring him to his knees. One night? A lifetime wouldn't be enough.

"I've been so blind," she murmured.

"Not anymore."

With the last pin gone, her hair tumbled in disarray about her shoulders. On a low growl of pleasure, he buried his hands in its soft luxuriance. He kissed her again, with all the reverence he felt. "You're so beautiful," he whispered.

She moaned against his lips and plucked at his shirt with an unashamed impatience that stoked his need. Panting he pulled away to tug his shirt over his head.

Her gaze fixed on his bare torso, and the salacious way she licked her lips sent another pulse of heat shuddering through him. "It's a sin to cover you up."

His laugh held a hint of bashfulness. "Why, thank you."

Expression intent, she placed her hands on his chest. He trembled as she stroked his shoulders and pectorals and belly. For a woman who had been in a hurry, she suddenly seemed to have all the time in the world. Just when he was ready to move a little faster, damn it. Still, her touch created its own joy. Torment, too, perhaps, but definitely joy. His skin burned under her lingering exploration. She curled her fingers in the light covering of hair on his chest, and the sting of fingernails made his blood simmer.

With a sigh, she moved closer, trailing kisses over his collarbone and lower. When her lips grazed his nipple, the simmer turned fierce. His breath hissed out.

With visible reluctance, she raised her head. "You don't like it?"

He laughed softly and plunged a hand into her hair, holding her for a quick kiss. "You take me to paradise."

"Good," she said, and returned to torturing him.

He endured her predations in a lather of barely restrained hunger, until those clever, seeking hands found his cock. "Devil take you," he grunted, catching her.

"I want to see you." She slid one hand free of his hold and flattened her palm against the front of his trousers. "Don't make me wait."

"Damn it," he bit out as he went up in flames. His cock, already hard, swelled and the ache in his balls made him grit his teeth. He reached down to shape her touch around where he needed her.

"Silas…" she sighed.

That shivery little sound goaded him on. He crashed his mouth into hers for a ferocious kiss, then went to work undressing her. He'd worried that she might need coaxing, but she was with him every step. To his gratification, she made no secret of her lusty enjoyment of his touch. After these bitter months, her willingness was twice as sweet. Her encouragement and audacity proved a potent mixture, making his hands shake as he unfastened her pretty yellow gown.

The dress slipped to the floor with a whisper of fabric. His animal self demanded that he push her onto the bed and climb on top of her. The soul that had spent more than a year starving for her told him to tarry, to notice, to remember.

So he lingered to take in the glory of Caro in filmy white corset and petticoat. A delighted smile curved his lips. "You look like a naughty milkmaid."

She laughed and shook the heavy fall of hair back from her face. With a naturalness that made his heart expand, she turned and presented her back, lifting her hair out of the way.

He kissed the curve of her shoulder, and set to removing the last barriers between them. Something of his deftness returned and soon clothing lay scattered around them. He nipped a line down her neck and across her nape.

"Ooh, Silas, I like that," she whispered in a husky voice that tested his control.

He breathed deeply, capturing the fragrance of her skin. Their turbulent encounter in his greenhouse had been too hurried and furious for him to appreciate the splendid details of his beloved. The precise texture of her silky hair. The tremulous, erratic catch of her breath. Her essence: warm, flowery, female. He could write sonnets to that scent.

He ran his teeth along a tendon in her neck until she gasped with pleasure. His hands traced her slender back to where gauzy fabric teased him with hints of curved buttocks and lovely legs. He slipped her drawers down and rested his hands on her supple waist as she stepped free of them.

At last, at last she was naked. Naked, except for her stockings gartered at the knee and the pretty yellow satin slippers with the ribbons around her neat ankles. He muffled an agonized groan. His need, already incandescent, burned hotter by degrees. He took an instant to thank whatever powers had ordained that she came to him.

"Shall I turn around?"

He heard a tremor of uncertainty. "Not yet."

Delaying the moment tantalized them both. The sight of her bare back and bottom made him power-fully aroused. She'd looked beguiling in corset and petticoat. Now that she was all but naked except for those come-hither stockings, she was irresistible. He needed a moment to shore up his restraint or Caro would find herself unceremoniously taken, never mind his best intentions.

Caro shifted from one foot to the other. "I feel a little awkward," she muttered.

"You look like a dream," he grated out, ripping in a frenzy at what remained of his clothing.

At last his bedamned trousers were off. Gently he touched her shoulder and drew her to face him. He knew by now that she wouldn't pretend coyness. Even so, astounded pleasure jolted him when her attention brazenly dropped to his cock, thick and erect.

"Good heavens," she said in blatant admiration.

Silas hardly heard her. He was too busy drinking in the sight of her body.

Caro was all feminine curves and pearly white skin. From her ruffled dark head to her elegant narrow feet, she was the loveliest creature he'd ever seen. She offered him a universe of marvels to explore. Lush breasts with dark pink nipples. Pale stomach with a mysterious little navel. Feathery dark curls hiding her sex.

He'd wanted her for so long, this generosity was too much. He swallowed to ease a desert-dry throat, but still his words emerged as a croak. "You are beyond exquisite."

He reached out almost hesitantly to cup one breast, testing its delectable weight in his palm. She sighed and pressed forward. She seemed too perfect for mortal man's possession. But he meant to take her and hold her and cherish her, until she ached to stay with him forever.

He delicately took her beaded nipple between his lips, tasting her sweetness. She groaned in encouragement and arched forward, burying her hands in his hair and bringing him closer. He drew harder on her breast, rewarded with another quivering sigh.

Hunger surged with invincible command. Fever overwhelmed everything but carnal need and he lost himself in adoring her beautiful body. Kissing all of her he could reach. Stroking her creamy skin. Discovering where she liked him to touch her. Oh, what delightful exploration.

Each second heightened his craving. He had to taste her or go mad. Gently he edged her backward until she bumped into the bed.

"Lie back," he said hoarsely. Without waiting for an answer, he caught her shoulders and set her on the mattress.

"Silas, what—" she began as he dropped to kneel between her splayed legs like a worshipper at an altar.

"Trust me," he said, catching her knees to prevent her instinctive withdrawal. Her scent surrounded him so that with every breath, she became more a part of him.

She propped herself on her elbows and surveyed him with a question in her heavy-lidded eyes. "This seems...wicked."

Her shyness filled his heart with tenderness. "I hope so."

"You can...see me."

Deliberately he looked down at the slick pink folds between her slender legs. His determination to claim that secret part of her pounded in his veins. "You're lovely everywhere."

She shifted again, more with self-consciousness than any need to escape, he was sure. "Nobody has ever…"

"You'll like it."

She frowned. "I'd better."

Her sudden imperiousness amused him. "Later, you can return the favor."

He waited to appreciate her dawning comprehension of his meaning. Then he bent to kiss her sex. A torrent of intoxicating impressions flooded his senses. The silky slide of his tongue against her most intimate place. The rich, humid scent. The hot, salty taste. The soft friction of curls against his face as he discovered every luscious dip and rise.

He licked her slowly, basking in her liquid response. Then he drew hard on the center of her pleasure. She cried out sharply. Pulling his hair, she wriggled against his invading mouth. The faint pain intensified his enjoyment, like a hint of tartness in an apple. Spreading her legs to give him greater access, he pressed further. Ruthlessly he speared his tongue into her, tasting more deeply. She released a long shuddering moan that sounded like the music of heaven.

He returned to teasing that sensitive little pearl of flesh, until she writhed like a mad creature. When he took her in his mouth, her broken cry rang out and her thighs clamped around his shoulders. He lapped at her, relishing her unabashed pleasure.

After an eon of quaking delight, her hands fell away from his hair to lie loose and open on the sheets at her sides. Her legs relaxed and she stretched panting upon the bed.

At last he looked up from her delicious mysteries. Her face was pale and transfigured. Her reddened lips curved in a faint reminiscent smile. Humbled by what she gave him so freely, he softly kissed each quivering thigh. Her beauty etched itself into his heart.

For months he'd imagined having her at his command, but the power of the emotion throbbing beneath his raging desire surprised him. It was mostly gratitude, spiced with unconditional love. He looked along Caro's graceful body to her unforgettable face, and recognized that she gave his life a center the way nothing else ever had.

Gently he untied her slippers and drew away her stockings. Impatience thundering in his blood, he arranged her across the sheets, pliant and rosy and warm. She made a sleepy protest as he rolled her into the middle of the bed, then opened her eyes when he rose above her on his arms.

"That was lovely," she murmured, eyes dark and weighted with satisfaction—and surprise.

"Not as lovely as you," he whispered fervently. He lowered into a kiss, rubbing his cock on her stomach, letting her know without words that he was ready.

Desire vibrated around them like beating wings, demanding satisfaction. She curled soft arms around his bare back. Her legs parted so sweetly to frame his hips.

When he lifted his head, she met his eyes, and her smile held no trace of shadow, only sensual welcome. "I want a lover, Lord Stone. I believe you might be suitable. Do you feel yourself up to the position?"

He pressed down more purposefully. The world shrank to a translucent sphere containing Caro Beaumont and him in a bed on a windy night. Extending these last seconds before his body slid into hers only built anticipation. "That's a terrible joke."

"If you require wit in a mistress, I'm afraid you must look elsewhere."

He laughed softly, delighted at her humor. More delighted that she admitted she was his mistress. She'd consent to more, once he'd answered all her doubts. If convincing her involved heady interludes like this, he couldn't begrudge the delay.

"Thank you, but I'll make do with the mistress I have. After all, if she's using her tongue to pleasure me, I can't complain if she's not using it to dazzle me with humor."

"Sensible," she said faintly. The opaque shine of her eyes hinted she approached a point where talking was no longer enough.

Silas kissed her lips, then bent to suckle her nipple. Her breath emerged in a voluptuous sigh. He nuzzled at her neck and slipped one hand between her legs. She was still wet, and his finger slid smoothly into her. Her muscles clenched against the incursion.

He stroked her gently, watching her expression change as she became accustomed to his touch. He withdrew at a leisurely pace, relishing the tantalizing glide. Then he slid two fingers into her, moving in and out until her eyes widened with heightening arousal.

She dragged him down for another kiss, clumsy and eager, then framed his face with unsteady hands. "Take me, Silas."

He shook his head and poured every ounce of the love he felt into his smile. "No, take *me*, Caro."

Before Caroline could question that response, Silas shifted and she felt a seeking pressure between her legs. Spreading her thighs wider, she tilted her hips. She burned to feel him inside her. Only he could answer her frantic longing.

He moved deeper. To her surprise, his entry stretched her to the point of discomfort. A soft whimper escaped her and he stopped, looking down at her with the familiar care. "Caro?"

She made herself smile and hooked her hands over his shoulders. "It's been a long time."

And Silas was so much...bigger than Freddie. Lord Stone was built on monumental lines. She recalled that stunning moment when she'd first seen him naked. She'd been nervous—and sinfully thrilled.

His expression softened and she read love in his hazel eyes. She realized with surprise that he'd watched her with the eyes of love for months.

"I'm sure you'll remember what to do." Laughter warmed his voice despite his rough breathing.

"You might need to remind me," she said, overwhelmingly conscious of his hard weight. She shifted again and he edged further. When he kissed her, she tasted passion. And love. It seemed Silas's love was inescapable.

Of course it was. Here she lay beneath him, and his love was the very air she breathed, along with the rich, musky male scent that fired her senses. She waited again for the old fear of captivity to rise. Surely if she was to feel trapped, now was the moment. But joined to this marvelous man, it was impossible to feel anything but treasured. And avid for the ultimate union.

She angled toward him. "Don't stop. I want you so much."

I love you so much.

"Oh, my darling," he whispered.

This time when he kissed her, she responded with all the emotion crammed unspoken in her heart. He raised his head and stared down at her with a question in his eyes—he'd notice the difference—but she bit his shoulder and rose to take him into her body.

Just as her heart flowered with love, her body flowered into delight. As he slid into her, his shuddering sigh expressed his happiness. Her fingers gripped his shoulders as he began to move. Hard, decisive thrusts that branded him on her heart as indelibly as a chisel carved wood. Swiftly her pleasure began to swell in great, engulfing waves. Over and over he plunged into her, hammering her into accepting his love.

Gasping Caroline ran her hands down the sleek skin of his back, feeling the muscles tighten and release with every stroke. She dug her fingers into the hard globes of his buttocks, encouraging him to go deeper and further and harder. Hot, restless, needy, she pressed upward.

"More," she gasped.

Despite his fierce possession, a broken laugh escaped him. "You're a demanding wench."

Catching her hip with one hand, he lifted her. All pretense at control disintegrated. He kissed her on the mouth and she responded savagely, using teeth and tongue. She was desperate for relief from this endless striving toward an unreachable pinnacle.

He circled his hips, plunged deep, and sudden fire split the night. She cried out again and sank her nails into his flanks. As roaring flame gushed through her, he groaned and bucked, flooding her. She lay quaking with wonder in his arms and knew she never wanted to be anywhere else as long as she lived.

Caroline only slowly floated down from that miraculous space caught in the light between stars. Her heart beat like a thousand drums and her blood pumped through her veins like hot honey. The world she inhabited was sweet as sugar, bright as sunlight.

Silas slumped in exhaustion, burying his face in her shoulder. His crushing weight made it impossible for Caroline to snatch a full breath. But, for once, in a good way. Her body ached from the vigorous loving in a way it never had after Freddie's desultory attentions.

And she was happier than she'd ever been before.

She sucked in a breath and blinked away the tears springing to her eyes.

Silas rose onto his elbows and glanced down at her. A frown wrinkled his brow. "Caro? Did I hurt you?"

"No," she said in a choked voice. After such a transcendent union, a woman should be proud and elated. Instead Caroline felt like a pathetic puddle of confused emotion. She untangled a hand from his hair and wiped roughly at her eyes. More idiotic tears welled. "It was wonderful. You were wonderful."

"Yet here you are, sobbing in my arms," he muttered. "You're obviously as happy as a dog with two tails."

She pushed at him until he rolled away, breaking the connection between them. Immediately she missed him. "I'm fine."

He turned onto his side and caught the trembling hand she clenched against his chest. "That sounds more like the woman I love. The minute she says she's fine, I know I'm in trouble. Tell me what's wrong."

She studied that beautiful, clever face that she should have long ago known would prove her downfall. "You wouldn't understand."

"Try me."

"I'm not sure even I understand."

His lips stretched in a smile so warm that it made her toes curl against the sheets. "Emotions are bewildering beasts, aren't they?"

"Yes," she agreed, reluctantly smiling back. His smile gave her the courage to speak. "I'm feeling at such a loss. I hardly know where to turn. I've never…never known anything like what just happened between us. Freddie wasn't a bad man, but we were a bad match. I did my duty by him and he did his duty by me, but it was a sour, barren bargain."

"No joy?"

Surprised, her vision filled with Silas, naked and virile beside her, instead of the ghosts of her lonely past. Perhaps he might understand after all. "Not one scrap of joy. Whereas what we did was—"

"Alight with joy."

"Yes."

"And now you regret all the wasted years."

"Of course I do." She freed her hand and sat up against the pillows, pulling the sheet over her breasts with belated self-consciousness. "I regret that in ten years of marriage, I experienced no satisfaction with my husband."

"I'm sorry. You're made for pleasure. It wasn't your fault."

Her mouth flattened, even as his description soothed her. "Some of it was. I was an unloving wife and Freddie knew it. Although the outside world would have looked at our match and wondered what I had to complain about. After all, however oblivious he was to anything beyond the estate boundaries, Freddie was kind and faithful and steadfast. It could have been worse."

"And every day, your spirit died a little more." Silas moved up on the pillows to brush back a strand of hair clinging to her damp cheek. "Don't discount the truth of your unhappiness. That only makes it worse. Hell is two incompatible people glued together for life."

"The definition of marriage," she said bitterly.

"The definition of an unhappy marriage." He leaned over her, his splendid shoulders creating their own horizon. His gaze was searching. "Who are you in love with, Caroline?"

She shrank away, would have run if he hadn't caught her wrist. "Don't ask me."

"I have to," he said gently, turning his grip into a caress as he stroked her, making her wayward pulse hop and skip under his dancing fingers. "Who, Caro?"

Her eyes narrowed on him as she struggled to

summon the exasperation his prying would once have sparked. "Naturally you think I'm in love with you."

The promise of another smile creased the corners of his eyes. "You know I love you."

She made a despairing gesture. "I don't want you to love me."

Self-derision lit his eyes. "Believe me, I didn't want to love you either."

Startled she surveyed him. It hadn't occurred to her that Silas, too, might have struggled against falling in love. "You didn't?"

His laugh was short. "Good God, no. I had the perfect life, diverting, self-indulgent, hedonistic. Then one day I met a widowed friend of my sister's, and that was the end of all my gallivanting."

"I want to do some gallivanting before I'm old," she said in a subdued voice, telling her heart it would *not* dissolve into mush at his declaration.

His face filled with such tenderness that her heart dissolved anyway. "You could gallivant with me."

He stroked her jaw with more of that melting tenderness. Dear heaven above, she was in terrible trouble here. She'd cried not just because she finally knew what Freddie's discontented wife had missed. She'd cried because Silas's possession had owned her so completely that she feared she'd never be free again.

And for over eleven years, freedom had been her goal, her only hope of happiness.

"Stop tempting me, Silas," she said thickly.

"Never. Tell me who you love."

"You know," she mumbled, avoiding those keen eyes that saw too much.

"I hope." His gentleness was more powerful than an army.

She sighed and looked directly at him. His dear, intriguing face was grave. "Oh, devil take you, you awful man. Of course I'm in love with you."

Silas stared down into his beloved's lovely, sulky face as a tide of elation flooded him.

"Don't look so pleased with yourself," Caroline said huskily.

"But I am pleased with myself." The understatement to end all understatements. He stopped trying to hold back his grin. She loved him. More astonishing, she'd admitted it. On a night of wonders, this was the greatest wonder yet. He felt like dancing around the room in triumph, whooping and punching the air like a lunatic.

She didn't look nearly so uplifted. "Now you'll think you have the right to choose my friends and criticize my clothes and tell me what to do, and you'll turn into a growling bear if I smile at another man."

"Probably," he said cheerfully.

"And you'll imagine I've made promises to you."

"Haven't you?"

She sat straighter and regarded him like an adversary. The wariness sat oddly on her features when her hair cascaded around her naked shoulders and her lips were red and swollen from his kisses. "I won't be a chattel."

"And I won't be a tyrant."

Her expression remained doubtful. "Easy for you to say."

"Will you give me the chance to prove myself?" He moved in to kiss her. After an infinitesimal hesitation, she kissed him back with all the glorious passion he'd discovered tonight. By the time he raised his head, she was flat on her back and he curved over her in a damnably suggestive pose.

"If I listen to you much longer, I'll give up my dreams."

"Perhaps it's time for new dreams."

To his surprise, he saw she gave the idea serious consideration. "New dreams sound…appealing."

"I'll make sure they are."

"So what do we do now?" she asked, sounding more confused than belligerent. She lay warm and soft and loose-limbed under him, his dream lover.

Suggestively he tilted his hips forward. "If you give me a couple of minutes, we can do it all again."

She cast him an unimpressed look, although the pink in her cheeks indicated interest. "Not that."

"Time's a-wasting. You only offered me one night."

Her lips quirked. "You don't expect me to believe you'll abide by that."

Silas didn't smile back. "Let me make a deal with you, sweetheart."

He must convince her to stay with him. Of course, he had the great advantage that she loved him. But that mightn't be enough. Silas cursed that idiot Freddie for giving her such a sour view of marriage.

"What sort of deal?" She sounded mistrustful. Physically she'd given herself without reservation. And mentally she'd ventured a long way toward him tonight.

"You said one night."

"I did."

"Then let's take our affair one night at a time." He didn't add that one night after another, year after year, totaled a lifetime.

She stared up at him, troubled. "Can you bear that? The uncertainty of it."

If she loved him, he wasn't uncertain at all. He was sure, and he believed that soon she would be, too. He shifted again, letting her feel his heavy readiness. "The compensations will make it worthwhile."

To his surprise, her arms crept around his neck. "I look forward to seeing you win this war, Silas."

Her lips were hot and ardent. By the time he raised his head, he was shaking with desire and poised between her legs.

"What was the question?" he asked huskily.

She glowed up at him. "Whatever it was, I think the answer is yes."

"I love you, Caro," he said, breath catching on a spike of poignant emotion.

"I love you, Silas." This time, the words emerged so smoothly that his heart leaped with hope. "So much."

He pressed his lips to hers once more to conceal his overwhelming relief and thankfulness. Elusive, fascinating, beloved Caroline Beaumont lay in his arms—and he swore by all that was holy, that was exactly where she'd stay. As his mistress, as his darling, and soon as his wife.

The dashing widow had met her match—and her true love.

ABOUT THE AUTHOR

ANNA CAMPBELL has written 10 multi award-winning historical romances for Grand Central Publishing and Avon HarperCollins, and her work is published in 22 languages. She has also written 21 bestselling independently published romances, including her series, The Dashing Widows and The Lairds Most Likely. Anna has won numerous awards for her Regency-set stories including Romantic Times Reviewers Choice, the Booksellers Best, the Golden Quill (three times), the Heart of Excellence (twice), the Write Touch, the Aspen Gold (twice) and the Australian Romance Readers Association's favorite historical romance (five times). Her books have three times been nominated for Romance Writers of America's prestigious RITA Award, and three times for Australia's Romantic Book of the Year. When she's not traveling the world seeking inspiration for her stories, Anna lives on the beautiful east coast of Australia.

Anna loves to hear from her readers. You can find her at:

Website: www.annacampbell.com

facebook.com/AnnaCampbellFans

twitter.com/AnnaCampbellOz

bookbub.com/authors/anna-campbell

goodreads.com/AnnaCampbell

ALSO BY ANNA CAMPBELL

Claiming the Courtesan

Untouched

Tempt the Devil

Captive of Sin

My Reckless Surrender

Midnight's Wild Passion

The Sons of Sin series:

Seven Nights in a Rogue's Bed

Days of Rakes and Roses

A Rake's Midnight Kiss

What a Duke Dares

A Scoundrel by Moonlight

Three Proposals and a Scandal

The Dashing Widows:

The Seduction of Lord Stone

Tempting Mr. Townsend

Winning Lord West

Pursuing Lord Pascal

Charming Sir Charles

Catching Captain Nash

Lord Garson's Bride

The Lairds Most Likely:

The Laird's Willful Lass

The Laird's Christmas Kiss

The Highlander's Lost Lady

Christmas Stories:

The Winter Wife

Her Christmas Earl

A Pirate for Christmas

Mistletoe and the Major

A Match Made in Mistletoe

The Christmas Stranger

Other Books:

These Haunted Hearts

Stranded with the Scottish Earl

TEMPTING MR TOWNSEND

(The Dashing Widows Book 2)

Beauty...

Fenella, Lady Deerham has rejoined society after five years of mourning her beloved husband's death at Waterloo. Now she's fêted as a diamond of the first water and London's perfect lady. But beneath her exquisite exterior, this delicate blond beauty conceals depths of courage and passion nobody has ever suspected. When her son and his school friend go missing, she vows to find them whatever it takes. Including setting off alone in the middle of the night with high-handed bear of a man, Anthony Townsend.

Will this tumultuous journey end in more tragedy? Or will the impetuous quest astonish this Dashing Widow with a breathtaking new love, and life with the last man she ever imagined?

And the Beast?

When Anthony Townsend bursts into Lady Deerham's fashionable Mayfair mansion demanding the return of his orphaned nephew, the lovely widow's beauty and spirit turn his world upside down. But surely such a refined and aristocratic creature will scorn a rough, self-made man's courtship, even if that man is now one of the richest magnates in England. Especially after he's made such a woeful first impression by barging into her house and accusing her of conniving with the runaways. But when Fenella insists on sharing the desperate search for the boys, fate offers Anthony a chance to play the hero and change her mind about him.

Will reluctant proximity convince Fenella that perhaps Mr. Townsend isn't so beastly after all? Or now that their charges are safe, will Anthony and Fenella remain forever opposites fighting their attraction?

WINNING LORD WEST

(The Dashing Widows Book 3)

All rakes are the same! Except when they're not...

Spirited Helena, Countess of Crewe, knows all about profligate rakes; she was married to one for nine years and still bears the scars. Now this Dashing Widow plans a life of glorious freedom where she does just what she wishes – and nobody will ever hurt her again.

So what is she to do when that handsome scoundrel Lord West sets out to make her his wife? Say no, of course. Which is fine, until West focuses all his sensual skills on changing her mind. And West's sensual skills are renowned far and wide as utterly irresistible...

Passionate persuasion!

Vernon Grange, Lord West, has long been estranged from his headstrong first love, Helena Nash, but he's always regretted that he didn't step in to prevent her disastrous marriage.

Now Helena is free, and this time, come hell or high water, West won't let her escape him again.

His weapon of choice is seduction, and in this particular game, he's an acknowledged master. Now that he and Helena are under one roof at the year's most glamorous house party, he intends to counter her every argument with breathtaking pleasure. Could it be that Lady Crewe's dashing days are numbered?

PURSUING LORD PASCAL

(The Dashing Widows Book 4)

Golden Days...

Famous for her agricultural innovations, Amy, Lady
Mowbray has never had a romantical thought in her life.
Well, apart from her short-lived crush on London's
handsomest man, Lord Pascal, when she was a brainless 14-
year-old. She even chose her late husband because he owned
the best herd of beef cattle in England!

But fate steps in and waltzes this practical widow out of her
rustic retreat into the glamour of the London season. When
Pascal pursues her, all her adolescent fantasies come true.
Those fantasies turn disturbingly adult when grown-up
desire enters the equation. Amy plunges headlong into a
reckless affair that promises pleasure beyond her wildest
dreams – until she discovers that this glittering world hides
damaging secrets and painful revelations set to break a
country girl's tender heart.

All that glitters...

Gervaise Dacre, Lord Pascal needs to marry money to save his estate, devastated after a violent storm. He's never much liked his reputation as London's handsomest man, but it certainly comes in handy when the time arrives to seek a rich bride. Unfortunately, the current crop of debutantes bores him silly, and he finds himself praying for a sensible woman with a generous dowry.

When he meets Dashing Widow Amy Mowbray, it seems all his prayers have been answered. Until he finds himself in thrall to the lovely widow, and his mercenary quest becomes dangerously complicated. Soon he's much more interested in passion than in pounds, shillings and pence. What happens if Amy discovers the sordid truth behind his whirlwind courtship? And if she does, will she see beyond his original, selfish motives to the ardent love that lies unspoken in his sinful heart?

CHARMING SIR CHARLES

(The Dashing Widows Book 5)

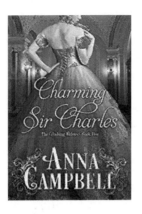

Matchmaking mayhem in Mayfair!

Sally Cowan, Countess of Norwood, spent ten miserable years married to an overbearing oaf. Now she's free, she plans to have some fun. But before she kicks her heels up, this Dashing Widow sets out to launch her pretty, headstrong niece Meg into society and find her a good husband.

When rich and charming Sir Charles Kinglake gives every sign that he can't get enough of Meg's company, Sally is delighted to play chaperone at all their meetings. Charles is everything that's desirable in a gentleman suitor. How disastrous, when over the course of the season's most elegant house party, Sally realizes that desire is precisely the name of the game. She's found her niece's perfect match—but she wants him for herself!

There are none so blind as those who will not see...

From the moment Sir Charles Kinglake meets sparkling Lady Norwood, he's smitten. He courts her as a gentleman should—dancing with her at every glittering ball, taking her to the theatre, escorting her around London. Because she's acting as chaperone to her niece, that means most times, Meg accompanies them. The lack of privacy chafes a man consumed by desire, but Charles's intentions are honorable, and he's willing to work within the rules to win the wife he wants.

However when he discovers that his careful pursuit has convinced Sally he's interested in Meg rather than her, he flings the rules out the window. When love is at stake, who cares about a little scandal? It's time for charming Sir Charles to abandon the subtle approach and play the passionate lover, not the society suitor!

Now with everything at sixes and sevens, Sir Charles risks everything to show lovely Lady Norwood they make the perfect pair!

CATCHING CAPTAIN NASH

(The Dashing Widows Book 6)

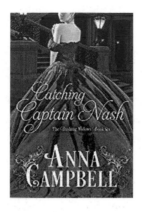

Home is the sailor, home from the sea...

Five years after he's lost off the coast of South America,
presumed dead, Captain Robert Nash escapes cruel captivity,
and returns to London and the bride he loves, but barely
knows. When he stumbles back into the family home, he's
appalled to find himself gate-crashing the party celebrating
his wife's engagement to another man.

This gallant naval officer is ready to take on any challenge;
but five years is a long time, and beautiful, passionate
Morwenna has clearly found a life without him. Can he win
back the wife who gave him a reason to survive his ordeal?
Or will the woman who haunts his every thought remain
eternally out of reach?

Love lost and found? Or love lost forever?

Since hearing of her beloved husband's death, Morwenna

Nash has been mired in grief. After five bleak years without him, she must summon every ounce of courage and determination to become a Dashing Widow and rejoin the social whirl. She owes it to her young daughter to break free of old sorrow and find a new purpose in life, even if that means accepting a loveless marriage.

It's a miracle when Robert returns from the grave, and despite the awkward circumstances of his arrival, she's overjoyed that her husband has come back to her at last. But after years of suffering, he's not the handsome, laughing charmer she remembers. Instead he's a grim shadow of his former dashing self. He can't hide how much he still wants her—but does passion equal love?

Can Morwenna and Robert bridge the chasm of absence, suffering and mistrust, and find their way back to each other?

LORD GARSON'S BRIDE

(The Dashing Widows Book 7)

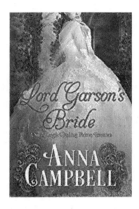

Lord Garson's dilemma.

Hugh Rutherford, Lord Garson, loved and lost when his fiancée returned to the husband she'd believed drowned. In the three years since, Garson has come to loathe his notoriety as London's most famous rejected suitor. It's high time to find a bride, a level-headed, well-bred lady who will accept a loveless marriage and cause no trouble. Luckily he has just the candidate in mind.

A marriage of convenience...

When Lady Jane Norris receives an unexpected proposal from her childhood friend Lord Garson, marriage to the handsome baron rescues her from a grim future. At twenty-eight, Jane is on the shelf and under no illusions about her attractions. With her father's death, she's lost her home and faces life as an impecunious spinster. While she's aware

Garson will never love again, they have friendship and goodwill to build upon. What can possibly go wrong?

...becomes very inconvenient indeed.

From the first, things don't go to plan, not least because Garson soon finds himself in thrall to his surprisingly intriguing bride. A union grounded in duty veers toward obsession. And when the Dashing Widows take Jane in hand and transform her into the toast of London, Garson isn't the only man to notice his wife's beauty and charm. He's known Jane all her life, but suddenly she's a dazzling stranger. This isn't the uncomplicated, pragmatic match he signed up for. When Jane defies the final taboo and asks for his love, her impossible demand threatens to blast this convenient marriage to oblivion.

Once the dust settles, will Lord Garson still be the man who can only love once?

Made in the USA
Middletown, DE
11 December 2019

80508104R00120